Follow Your Star

Follow Your Star

Jennifer Bohnet

ROBERT HALE · LONDON

© Jennifer Bohnet 2009
First published in Great Britain 2009

ISBN 978-0-7090-8909-4

Robert Hale Limited
Clerkenwell House
Clerkenwell Green
London EC1R 0HT

www.halebooks.com

The right of Jennifer Bohnet to be identified as
author of this work has been asserted by her
in accordance with the Copyright, Designs and
Patents Act 1988

2 4 6 8 10 9 7 5 3 1

Typeset in 11½/16pt Palatino
by Derek Doyle & Associates, Shaw Heath
Printed in Great Britain by the MPG Books Group, Bodmin and King's Lynn

CHAPTER ONE

'Nanette, this has been just a perfect day. You are so clever to have found this place for us. I can't thank you enough.' Vanessa hugged her friend tightly.

Nanette and Vanessa were standing by the entrance to The Old Folly. Set in the middle of a snowdrop-covered field with views tumbling down the Devonshire countryside towards a distant river sparkling in the late afternoon winter sunshine, it had proved to be an ideal venue for Vanessa and Ralph's wedding.

Nanette smiled at her friend and employer.

'I must admit to being a bit worried about organizing your big day. It's been such a long time since I've done anything like it.' She paused. 'I did wonder whether I was still up to it.'

'You did a great job. No problems at all,' Vanessa said.

'You were a beautiful bride,' Nanette said.

'Right, enough of this mutual admiration society,' Vanessa said. 'I need to talk to you urgently.'

'Can't it wait until you return? You are only away for the weekend. Incidentally, you have to leave in about ten minutes,' Nanette said, glancing at her watch. 'Surely Ralph must be wondering where his new wife is?'

'He knows I'm with you. It's important for me to talk to you before we leave. I have to ask you something.'

Vanessa glanced at Nanette.

'You know that Ralph has got this big filming project lined up in the Amazon?'

'Yes. He was telling me earlier it's his biggest project yet,' Nanette said.

'He wants me to go with him. We'd have a week's belated honeymoon in Brazil and then I'd become part of his team filming the documentary in the rain forest.'

'For the whole of the five months?'

Vanessa nodded.

'How do you feel about being away for so long? What about the twins and your business— Oh,' this, as realization dawned. 'You want me to step into your shoes while you're away?' Nanette took a deep breath.

'Looking after the twins, fine I'm used to that – but running the business? I don't think I can do it.' Nanette shook her head. 'Organizing today with the help of your office, is one thing, running your business in your absence, would be totally different.'

She looked at Vanessa anxiously. 'You know I haven't done any PA work since. . . .' She shrugged and didn't finish the sentence. 'I did think after organizing today, I'd ask if I could come in and do a regular stint in the office to get me back into the swing of things but being in charge—'

'No, I don't want you to run the business,' Vanessa interrupted. 'Caroline is more than happy to look after that side of things for me – she's been taking on more and more responsibilities recently anyway. But I do want you to carry on looking after the twins for me.'

Nanette breathed a sigh of relief.

'Of course I'll look after the twins while you're away, but five months is a long time. What happens if there's an emergency? Do I have full responsibility? What about Mathieu?'

There was a pause as Vanessa fiddled with the sprays of freesias pinned to her wedding dress, before she looked directly at Nanette and added quietly, 'I want you to look after the twins in Monaco.'

Vanessa held her hands up in a conciliatory gesture as Nanette looked at her aghast.

'I know, I know. You vowed never to go back. And I promised you wouldn't have to. But Mathieu has agreed to have the twins for six months on condition that you go too and look after them like you do here for me. He says he's too busy to become a school-gate-dad.'

Nanette turned away and watched silently as an all-enveloping mist began to rise from the river and drift up towards the medieval Folly. The day was turning cold as the last rays of sunlight vanished.

Damp air began to swirl around them as the reassuring presence of the old building became shrouded in the mist. Nanette tried unsuccessfully to suppress a shivery shudder of apprehension at the very thought of returning to Monaco. Painful memories of a place she'd pushed into the darkest recess of her mind began to swirl into her consciousness.

'Can't Mathieu come over here?' she said desperately, turning back to face Vanessa. 'I'll willingly look after him and the twins here.'

Vanessa shook her head. 'Apparently not. He says it's

impossible for him to leave the country for so long. He's got some sort of business deal going through and needs to be there.'

Vanessa placed an arm around Nanette's shoulders.

'I realize I am asking a lot. I know how difficult it will be for you to even think about returning and if you can't face it, I will understand. So will Ralph,' Vanessa said. 'But will you please consider the idea while Ralph and I are away this weekend?'

Patsy, her sister, was waiting as Nanette shepherded the twins, Pierre and Olivia, off the train later that evening.

'Hi. Everything go according to plan? Good. That's a lovely frock you're wearing, Olivia. Did you enjoy being your mum's bridesmaid? Of course you did, silly question that. And you, Pierre, how are you doing? The car's parked right outside; we should be home in fifteen minutes. I expect you're looking forward to supper – or did you fill up on wedding goodies?'

Listening to her, Nanette felt breathless. She was always amazed at the speed at which Patsy spoke and sometimes found it difficult to get a word in, let alone answer any questions. But Patsy was kindness itself and four years ago when she'd married Bryan, a local farmer, she'd settled into her role of farmer's wife like a born countrywoman.

'How are you? Any news? Think you've put on weight since I last saw you,' Nanette asked quickly, when Patsy finally took a breath.

'I'm fine. My news can wait until later. And talking of weight – you could do with putting on some, you're scrawnier than ever,' Patsy said, with sisterly bluntness. 'I hope you are eating properly – or has organizing the wedding stressed you out?'

Nanette didn't answer but sighed happily as they turned on to the track leading to Blackberry Farm. She was really looking forward to this weekend break. Life recently had been busier than she'd become accustomed to for the past couple of years and she was tired after all the excitement of planning the wedding.

She knew the twins always enjoyed themselves down here, and would disappear for hours at a time, exploring the woods and surrounding fields and helping Bryan around the farm, giving her some precious time to herself.

'How's Bryan's mum? Enjoying her new home?' Nanette asked, as they passed a pristine bungalow at the top of the lane.

'Think so. But you know Helen. Drove Bryan mad for the first week or two wanting shelves put up and cupboards moved but she's finally got it as she wants, although the kitchen will *never* be right – it's far too small! And, of course, she'll never like living there as much as she enjoyed the farmhouse – even though she moaned for years it was too big and draughty. She'll be joining us for lunch on Sunday so you are sure to hear all about the drawbacks of having to live in a modern bungalow.' Patsy smiled at her sister.

Once the twins had been fed and settled in their rooms, and Bryan was in the study working on the farm accounts, Nanette and Patsy made themselves comfortable in the sitting-room for a sisterly chat.

'Glass of wine to toast the happy couple?' Nanette asked, opening a bottle she'd brought from the reception.

'A small glass,' Patsy said. 'I shouldn't really, but I don't suppose a sip will hurt junior, Aunty.' She grinned mischievously at Nanette.

'Oh, congratulations,' Nanette said, hugging her sister. 'When's it due?'

'Late June early July. No definite date yet. But knowing my luck it will be right in the middle of haymaking. Can you be here? I really, really want you around. Helen is already threatening to move back up here to help out. Promise me you'll tell Vanessa you need to be here. You can bring the twins.' Patsy looked anxiously at Nanette.

'I'll be here,' Nanette promised. 'Even if Vanessa is still paddling her canoe up the Amazon I'll be here.'

'Vanessa's going up the Amazon?' For once Patsy seemed speechless.

'Yep,' and Nanette told her sister about Ralph's wish to make his new wife part of his film team. Patsy took it for granted that Nanette would be looking after the twins whilst Vanessa was away.

'You'll all be able to come down regularly. Oh, I'm really beginning to look forward to the next few months.'

Nanette shook her head.

'Afraid not, Patsy. Mathieu has agreed to have the twins to live with him while Vanessa's away.' She took a sip of wine before adding quietly, 'The only condition is I go with them.'

Patsy's eyes widened in incredulity.

'You're not serious? I know it's nearly three years ago and you've supposedly recovered from all the trauma, but are you strong enough to face things out there? You're bound to meet up with certain people; certain situations are going to bring back painful memories.'

'I know. I haven't agreed yet. My first reaction when Vanessa mentioned it this afternoon was no, no, no.' Nanette swirled the wine in her glass thoughtfully. 'But Vanessa's been very good to me – I owe her so much. I'd feel as though I'd let her down if I don't agree. She desperately wants to go with Ralph.'

'I'm sure she'll understand if you say you can't do it though,' Patsy said. 'Surely Mathieu could find someone local to help look after the twins for a few hours each day after school. And doesn't his father, what's his name, Jean-Claude, live nearby? I'm sure he'd be delighted to have some bonding time with his grandchildren. Personally I don't think you need to go at all.'

Nanette looked at her sister. 'I was thinking that maybe I do need to go – return to the scene of the crime as it were. Being airlifted out so quickly there were a lot people I didn't get to say goodbye to.'

'Not many of them have been in touch with you since though, have they?' Patsy demanded. 'Not even the Heel, despite insisting he was acting in your best interests at the time.'

Nanette flinched. 'Perhaps by going I can finally close that particular chapter in my life,' she said quietly.

Patsy shook her head. 'Oh Nanette. If you feel like that I don't know what to say or suggest. I just don't want you being hurt again. I'm afraid you'll find going back a lot harder than you expect. I only hope you can cope with any recriminations that occur. Just promise me that if you do go and things get too difficult you'll come straight back here – with the twins if necessary.'

'Where else would I go?' Nanette said quietly. 'But what do I do if I don't agree to take the twins to Monaco? If I say no and Mathieu organizes some local help with the twins while Vanessa disappears up the Amazon, my job here vanishes.'

'Oh, come on, Nanette. Vanessa has always treated you as part of her family. That's not likely to change,' Patsy said. 'She'll probably offer to find you a job in the office. She's certainly not going to throw you out on the street.'

'I guess you're right.' Nanette sighed looking at her sister. 'Are you all right? You look a bit pale,' she said concerned.

Patsy put down her untouched glass of wine.

'Excuse me – don't know why it's called morning sickness, mine comes at all times,' and she disappeared in the direction of the bathroom. 'Back in a mo.'

An ashen Patsy reappeared a few minutes later.

'If you don't mind, I'm going to go to bed. We'll talk more tomorrow.'

Deciding to have an early night herself, Nanette followed her sister up the stairs. Unpacking the suitcase in her familiar bedroom tucked away in the eaves of the farmhouse, she remembered the weeks she'd spent here after being flown back from Monaco just days after her body and her successful career had been shattered.

It was here Vanessa had come to find her nearly three years ago. Walking into her room to cajole her back to life she'd said, 'You're looking better than the last time I saw you.'

'Considering I was still black and blue and various bits of me were swathed in bandages, that's not hard.' Nanette smiled. 'How are the twins? Your business?'

'Pierre and Olivia are fine and the business is really taking off,' Vanessa said. 'Mathieu has taken them to Disneyland for a few days. He was a lousy husband but I have to give him credit – he does try to be a good father. I just wish he hadn't decided to live in Monaco permanently. It makes access a bit complicated.'

Vanessa glanced at Nanette. 'How about you? Have you made any plans for your future yet?'

Nanette shook her head. 'No. I'm trying to find the courage to face the world again, but I can't decide which problem to tackle first: nowhere to live, no job and my savings rapidly disappearing.' She looked helplessly at Vanessa. 'I just don't know where to start. And on top of it all I feel such a fool.'

'Hey, you're not a fool. You were holding down a very busy and stressful job when the accident happened. If Zac Ewart had an ounce of decency in him, he'd have supported you, made sure you had a job to go back to, not dumped you before the case came to court.

'Honestly Nanette, I can't believe he behaved as he did. Talk about putting the boot in when you were down. You were engaged, for goodness sake. He should have stood by you.'

Nanette bit her lip as she listened to her friend and vainly tried to stop the tears flowing down her cheeks.

Vanessa, instantly contrite, put her arms around her friend.

'Nanette, I'm sorry. I didn't mean to upset you. It's just I get so mad on your behalf.'

There was a pause before she continued, 'Will you come and work for me?'

Nanette looked at her in surprise. 'You need a PA for the business?'

Vanessa shook her head. 'No. Caroline is doing a great job. What I need is a housekeeper and someone to help with the twins. I know it's not what you're trained for, but maybe a complete change for a while would be good? I have to be away a lot in the next few months and I need someone at home I can trust to look after the twins and generally take care of things.'

'You're not offering me a job out of pity?' Nanette asked.

'Definitely not. I'm trying to juggle home and work and I'm desperate for some help. Being a single mum is difficult enough without trying to start and keep a business afloat. I need you Nanette.'

'What happens about getting the twins to Monaco to visit Mathieu? I couldn't face taking them there. I can't do the school run either now I've lost my licence,' Nanette added quietly.

'Mathieu will have to collect them. We'll sort something out so you don't have to go. As for the school run, we're only ten minutes away. Much better for them to walk anyway.

'I can't pay you a fortune but you'll have your own room, your keep – although you'll be in charge of the cooking! I thought it would help us both – you to get back on your feet and recover from recent events, and me because I will have someone I can trust utterly while I concentrate on this business and make it work.'

'Maybe we could try it for a couple of months? See how things work out,' Nanette said thoughtfully. 'Have to warn you though, I'm not a brilliant cook.'

'Great,' Vanessa said. 'School starts next week so how d'you feel about coming back with me tomorrow? You can settle in and have a few days to organize a routine.'

Patsy had fussed over her like a mother hen for the next twenty-four hours, worried that she wasn't ready to leave the sanctuary of the farm, but pleased that there was to be some purpose in her life again.

The couple of months' trial had gone quickly and Nanette, finding she enjoyed a domestic working environment more than she'd thought possible, had happily agreed to stay on permanently. It was certainly less stressful than her previous job as a PA to a Grand Prix team.

She adored looking after the twins and running the house, especially when Vanessa was away on one of her frequent business trips. It was like having her own home and children, something she'd always wanted – had imagined having by now, if only things had turned out differently.

Mathieu, Vanessa's ex-husband visited frequently much to the twins delight. Separated when the children were still tiny, he and Vanessa had managed to remain friends despite their differences and both did their best for the twins. Pierre and Olivia were now so used to the way their lives were divided between England and Monaco they simply accepted it as the way their particular family worked.

The sudden switching on of an outside light, brought Nanette out of her daydream and back to the present. Bryan was crossing the farmyard to do his final night-time check of the animals in the barn.

Thoughtfully, Nanette drew the curtains and turned to finish her unpacking. Could she really turn her back on everything Vanessa had done for her and refuse to help out in her current crisis? Besides, if she didn't agree to take the twins to Monaco where would that leave her?

Patsy was right when she said Vanessa treated her like family, but relatives had fallen out over less and Nanette dreaded the thought of losing contact with Vanessa and the twins simply because she refused to go to Monaco and face up to her past.

The smell of freshly percolating coffee greeted Nanette as she made her way down to the kitchen on Sunday morning.

Patsy was busy pushing sprigs of rosemary and cloves of garlic into a large leg of lamb ready to roast for lunch.

'Hi. Did you sleep well? The twins are helping Bryan feed the baby calves. Help yourself to coffee. You know where the cereals are. There's plenty of bread for toast. I'd offer you bacon and eggs but I can't stand the smell of bacon cooking at the moment.'

'Coffee and toast will be just fine. I'll do the vegetables for lunch afterwards, shall I?' Nanette asked.

'Thanks. Helen always insists on bringing the dessert so I don't have to worry she says. More like she doesn't like my pastry! I thought we could go for a walk after lunch – maybe take the twins down to the lake. Helen always likes Bryan to take her on a tour of the farm on Sunday afternoons like they used to when Albert was alive.' Patsy sighed.

'Honestly, Nanette, sometimes I could strangle the woman, but she does mean well I suppose. I thought when she finally moved out things would be better. She'd get an independent life again. Leave Bryan and me to our own devices a bit more.' Patsy shook her head. 'But nothing's really changed. She's still here every day on some pretence or other. And Sunday lunch up here every week has become something of a ritual. Not sure how I'm going to cope with the "grandmotherly" advice that is sure to be heaped on me. That's why I need you here as an ally when junior arrives.' Patsy glanced at her sister. 'Any closer to deciding what you're going to do?'

Nanette shook her head.

'No. Maybe the walk this afternoon will clear my head and I'll be able to think straight.'

Helen arrived just as Patsy placed the roast in the Rayburn

and immediately queried whether it would be cooked in time.

'I always had the meat in that range by ten o'clock at the latest. Ready for lunch at one on the dot. Still you young things abhor routines, don't you? Mind you, once the baby arrives you'll soon change your tune.'

'Helen, it's lovely to see you again,' Nanette said quickly before Patsy could respond to her mother-in-law's criticisms. 'How's life in your new home?'

'Different to what I've been used to, but I'm settling in nicely, thank you. Once Bryan finishes off a couple more little jobs I'll be really organized. Ready to devote my time to helping Patsy with the new addition.'

Helen slanted a look at Nanette.

'And you? Your memory back to normal now?' she asked briskly. 'I saw a picture in one of the Sunday papers recently of – oh what's his name? Your ex fiancé anyway. Had a blonde on his arm. Said something about them getting married. Zachary – that's his name.'

'I saw that photo too,' Nanette said quietly. 'As for my memory, I still have no recollection of certain things people tell me happened – maybe it's for the best,' she added, forcing a smile in Helen's direction. 'If you'll excuse me I'll just go check on the twins.'

Leaving the kitchen, Nanette mouthed an apologetic, 'Sorry – I'll see you later', at Patsy before closing the kitchen door behind her.

After a slightly strained lunch, Nanette, Patsy and the twins went for their planned walk down to the lake at the far end of the farm.

'I'm sorry Helen assumed your memory had returned to normal,' Patsy said quietly. 'And mentioned you-know-who.

I know you find both difficult to cope with.'

Nanette shook her head wearily. 'Don't worry. I wish my memory of that afternoon would return, but I'm beginning to believe it never will now. As for Zac, well, I can't hide from news about him for ever.'

Opening a heavy farm gate so that Patsy didn't have to climb over as the twins had done, Nanette said to her sister, 'Actually I think Helen's comments have helped me make up my mind. I can't run from the past for ever, so' – she took a deep breath – 'I'm going to tell Vanessa yes I will go to Monaco. At least Mathieu will be around if there are any problems with the twins and he'll be a friend for me too.'

Nanette could feel the wind tearing at her face as she frantically skied faster and faster down the mountainside. Adrenalin flowed through her veins as she heard the noise of the avalanche behind her gathering speed, devouring everything in its way. Her lungs forced a terror-stricken scream into the air. She couldn't die like this, she. . . !

'Nanette, Nanette, wake up. You're having one of your nightmares,' Patsy shook her gently.

A shudder went through Nanette's body as she came to.

'Here, have a sip.' Patsy handed her a glass of water. 'What was it this time? Another monster breaking into the house? An earthquake?'

Nanette shook her head. 'No. I was caught up in an avalanche.' She took a sip of the water as Patsy regarded her thoughtfully.

'It's been ages since you've had a nightmare.'

Nanette nodded. 'I know. I was hoping they'd finally

finished,' she said, her body still racked with shakes. 'The therapist was saying only last week that it was a good sign I'd gone for so long without one. Wonder what interpretation she'll put on tonight's little episode?' Nanette added through chattering teeth.

'The stress of planning the wedding? Or maybe the thought of returning to Monaco?' Patsy said, giving her sister a concerned glance. 'Are you cold? Shall I get you a hot water bottle?'

'No, thanks. I'll snuggle back under the duvet in a moment and I'll soon warm up,' and Nanette smiled at her sister. 'You go back to bed. Remember your condition. Don't want you with dark circles under your eyes tomorrow, or rather today. She glanced at the bedside clock. 'I'm sorry I woke you.'

'If you're sure you're OK,' Patsy said. 'I could stay with you for a bit?'

'I'm fine. Go back to bed,' Nanette ordered. 'But leave the light on please.'

Patsy glanced anxiously at her before leaving and closing the door.

Once she was alone, Nanette sat on the edge of the bed and took some deep breaths, trying to get her shaking body under control. It was never easy to banish the apprehension and terror that the nightmares brought.

Sitting there, watching a moth seemingly mesmerized by the bedside light, flying frantically round and round, Nanette's thoughts ricocheted in a similar manner over her latest nightmare.

These terrifying dreams had been an irregular part of her nights for nearly three years now. Ever since the car accident in which she – and Zachary Ewart – had nearly died.

The therapist, whom Vanessa had persuaded her to see when they began, had been right when she'd said they would happen less and less as time went on. But tonight's nightmare had been truly terrifying. As bad as any she'd ever had. Slowly, as she sat there, the shaking stopped and the feeling of devastation retreated into her subconscious. But she knew there had been an extra dimension tonight – something that had disappeared as she'd woken up.

As she'd hurtled down that slope in the path of the avalanche, screaming in terror, she hadn't been alone. A shadowy figure had been alongside urging her on.

'Faster, faster. Remember, remember. . . .'

Remember what? Despondently Nanette replayed the nightmare in her mind, trying to come up with some positive memory from the dream. But her brain refused to co-operate.

Wearily, she slipped under the duvet and reached out to turn off the light. Hopefully the rest of the night would pass peacefully. Now the decision was made and she was going to return to Monaco, she would need all her strength to cope with the coming weeks.

The Mediterranean was sparkling under a warm March sun as the plane landed and taxied along the landing strip of Nice Cote d'Azur airport that ran alongside the edge of the sea. Nanette took a deep breath.

After several weeks of frenzied preparations, Vanessa and Ralph had left for Brazil and she was finally back on French soil. Whatever the next few months had in store for her she could only pray that the turbulence of her past wouldn't intrude into the future.

She undid her seatbelt and began to gather their things

together. The twins were already on their feet excited at the prospect of the next part of the journey.

Walking through the arrivals hall Nanette put on her large sunglasses. She knew from experience that there was always the odd photographer, or even a group of paparazzi, lurking around the airport in the hope of snapping someone famous on their way out to the helicopter pad for transfer to Monaco.

She knew she was unlikely to be of any interest, but hiding her eyes behind the dark glass made her feel better.

But it wasn't the paparazzi who greeted her as she walked towards the helicopter check-in desk: it was a large billboard advertising the Monaco Grand Prix standing next to it. A smaller one alongside had a film-star-style close-up of the Heel's face and the words *'Is this Zac's year?'* emblazoned over it.

Nanette handed over their flight reservation tickets to the desk clerk, turning her back on the poster and trying to shut its image and the memories it evoked out of her mind.

'Great,' Pierre said excitedly. 'We'll be here this year for the Grand Prix. Do you think Dad will be able to get us some passes for the pit lane?'

'I shouldn't be surprised,' Nanette said, with a sinking feeling. She'd totally forgotten their time in Monaco would clash with the Grand Prix. That local hero Zachary Ewart would naturally be in town.

'Well, I don't want a ticket,' Olivia said. 'I hate the noise those cars make. It hurts my ears.'

Inwardly Nanette agreed with Olivia. The last thing she wanted too was a ticket to anything that involved Zachary Ewart.

The twins clambered happily into their seats in the

helicopter leaving Nanette to sit alongside the pilot. As the turbines screamed, the rotors beat the air and the helicopter took off in a rush of noise, Nanette took some deep, steadying breaths.

The pilot glanced at her sympathetically.

'First trip? You look a bit nervous. It's only fifteen minutes.'

Nanette shook her head. 'No. It's not my first trip but I am nervous.'

Staring out through the window at the coastline that had once been so familiar to her, Nanette didn't add that it wasn't the flight she was nervous about, but the direction her life was taking.

After landing at the heli-pad in Fontvielle, a downtown extension of Monaco built on reclaimed land, Nanette and the twins took a taxi to Mathieu's apartment on Boulevard Albert 1st overlooking the old port. Within minutes the twins were knocking on the door of Mathieu's ninth floor apartment.

To Nanette's surprise, it was his father, Jean-Claude, who opened the door to them.

'*Bonjour mes petits* and welcome,' he said, hugging the twins and giving Nanette a light kiss on each cheek.

'Where's Daddy?' Olivia asked disappointedly.

'He'll be here later, poppet,' Jean-Claude said. 'He's had to take care of some business this afternoon. You two can take your things through to your rooms while I show Nanette hers. Tea and biscuits on the balcony in ten minutes.'

Once the twins were safely out of earshot, Jean-Claude said to Nanette, 'Mathieu offers his apologies but something came up that he couldn't get out of. He hopes to be here later this evening. In the meantime, he's asked me to take care of things. Help you settle in, give you keys and things. And I'll stay tonight in case he doesn't get back.'

He picked up Nanette's suitcase.

'You haven't been to this apartment before, have you?'

Nanette shook her head. 'No, Mathieu had a place up in Monte Carlo itself the last time I was here. It was a lot smaller than this one.'

'Come on then, I'll show you around.'

The apartment with its five bedrooms, numerous bathrooms, large sitting-room with doors opening out on to the balcony was as sumptuous as any Nanette had ever been in. Fleetingly she wondered how Mathieu could afford such luxury, but maybe Jean-Claude, who she knew ran a successful business, had helped him out.

Her own room was charming – a mixture of French Provençal furnishings and modern pieces; it had its own balcony with a sea view and an en suite bathroom in marble.

'It's a very grand apartment,' she said slowly.

Jean-Claude smiled. 'I have a feeling having the twins living here for a few months will turn it into more of a home. Now, I'm sure Florence will have tea and biscuits ready on the balcony. Shall we join the twins?'

'Who is Florence?' Nanette asked, as they made their way back to the sitting-room.

'Mathieu's housekeeper.'

Nanette turned and looked at Jean-Claude in surprise.

'But that's partly what I thought *I* was here to be. Mathieu doesn't really need me if he's already got someone.'

'You're here simply to look after the twins – organize them when they are not at school.'

'But that's going to leave me with an awful lot of time on my hands,' Nanette protested. 'With nothing to do.'

Jean-Claude didn't answer. He simply raised his eyebrows at her quizzically.

'I'm sure you'll find plenty to do once you're settled in. Thank you, Florence, we'll manage now.'

Absentmindedly, Nanette accepted the cup of tea Jean-Claude handed her.

'I take it Vanessa and Ralph got away all right yesterday?' Jean-Claude asked.

Nanette nodded, forcing herself to concentrate.

'The twins and I went to Heathrow to wave them goodbye at the crack of dawn. They should be sleeping off their jet lag right now. Vanessa said she'd phone tonight to make sure everything was OK this end.'

'Nanette, Pierre wants to play with his computer game and I want to watch television in my room,' Olivia said. 'Can we?'

'Half an hour then it's bedtime,' Nanette agreed, and smiled as the twins dashed away.

'I have to talk to you,' Jean-Claude said.

Nanette looked at him in surprise as he hesitated.

'Nanette, can I be honest with you? I obviously didn't want to say anything in front of the twins, but I think you have a right to know. It's extremely unlikely that Mathieu will be here tonight.'

Nanette waited as a clearly agitated Jean-Claude ran his hands through his hair.

'I've spent most of this afternoon with my lawyers,' he said, 'trying to sort things out, but. . . .' and Jean-Claude shrugged unhappily as he looked at her.

There was a pause before he added, 'You see, Nanette, Mathieu hasn't been delayed by business: he's been arrested.'

CHAPTER TWO

Nanette was enjoying a coffee and a croissant early on Saturday morning at one of the cafés that edged the small Monaco flower and vegetable market, when her mobile rang.

'Hi, Patsy. Everything all right?' she asked quickly, seeing her sister's name on the screen.

'Yes. Just wondering how you are, as I haven't heard from you and I was worried,' her sister said.

'Everything's fine here now,' Nanette said.

'What do you mean *now*?' Patsy demanded. 'What's happened? Are the twins all right? Are you?'

Nanette hesitated. 'Mathieu wasn't here when I arrived. He'd been arrested.'

Quickly, before Patsy could draw breath, Nanette continued, 'He's out now. They kept him in for twenty-four hours before releasing him on bail. He has to report back once a week.'

'What's he done?'

'I don't know exactly. Something to do with his business,' Nanette said. 'Apparently all he said to Jean-Claude was, it's nothing to worry about and that he'd get it sorted.'

She didn't add that Jean-Claude was furious with his son for not asking him to put up the bail money. Instead an unnamed foreign business associate had stood surety.

'I'm sorry I haven't rung you before, but as you can imagine, trying to occupy the twins and keep the news of their father's arrest from them hasn't left a lot of time for anything else. Thankfully, Mathieu has taken them to Marineland today to give me a couple of free hours. And Jean-Claude is organizing a computer for them so they'll be able to follow Vanessa and Ralph's progress from this weekend.'

'Have you heard from them?'

'Only that they arrived safely in Brazil and are enjoying themselves. Their honeymoon will be over next weekend when they meet up with the documentary team and they begin work.'

'When do the twins start school?'

'Monday, so that's something else we've been busy doing: sorting clothes, buying books and stationery and back-packs big enough to carry everything. Honestly the amount of stuff they have to carry on a daily basis is unbelievable.'

'And you?' Patsy asked. 'How are you coping with being back in Monaco? Met up with anyone from your past yet?'

'If you mean, have I seen Zac the answer is no,' Nanette said. 'How's your morning sickness?'

'Slowing down, thank goodness,' Patsy said. 'I'd better go – Helen is about to arrive and if she realizes I'm on the phone to you I shall get a lecture about wasting Bryan's hard-earned money on foreign phone calls!'

'I'll ring you at the weekend,' Nanette said laughing. 'Take care.'

Thoughtfully she put the phone in her bag and looked around her at the colourful scene. Local housewives and Filipino servants with raffia baskets were busy doing their daily fresh vegetable shop and even at this early hour the walkway up to the palace was crowded with tourists.

It was hard to believe she'd been back in Monaco for nearly a week. If someone had told her last year that she would once again be living here, her immediate reaction would have been outright disbelief. The scars were still too sore to even contemplate returning.

But, having settled in, and despite the problems of the last few days, Nanette was beginning to enjoy being back.

She hadn't told Patsy, but last night Mathieu had taken her out to dinner, partly to apologize for not being there when she arrived and also because, 'I'd like to,' he'd said, with a disarming smile when suggesting it. . . .

The Italian restaurant he'd taken her to was hidden away in one of the back streets away from the tourist haunts.

'I'm so glad you decided you'd come with the twins,' Mathieu said, as they waited for their first course to arrive.

'Can't understand why you wanted me here really,' Nanette said. 'Florence lives in, and Jean-Claude seems more than happy to help look after the twins.'

'I thought it was important for Pierre and Olivia to have some sort of continuity in their lives. They are used to you looking after them when Vanessa is away – I just thought it would make things easier for them.'

He smiled at her and added, 'It certainly made things easier for me earlier in the week knowing that you were here with them when I had my spot of bother.'

There was a slight pause before he said quietly, 'I have to

confess to an ulterior motive too. I also hoped we could get to know each other better. That perhaps you could stop thinking of me as the twins' father and we could become better friends.'

The waiter had arrived with their starters at that moment and spared a surprised Nanette from responding. Afterwards Mathieu changed the conversation to more general things.

'It's the Tennis Masters Series soon,' he said. 'I remember you and Zac used to play a lot. I've been offered a pair of tickets for the opening day, would you like to come with me?'

'Oh please,' Nanette said, ignoring the flicker of pain at the mention of Zac. They had been passionate about tennis, both playing and watching.

'Good. I'll confirm the tickets before I go away next week.'

'Business trip, or pleasure?' she asked.

'A trip to Switzerland on business,' he said quietly. 'So long as the authorities don't prevent me leaving.'

'Are they likely to?'

He shrugged. 'I'm hoping they'll realize they've made a mistake in the next couple of days and everything will be sorted out. I'm not the man they want.'

'Do you know who is?' Nanette asked quietly.

Mathieu had nodded. 'Oh yes.'

As they finished their meal and prepared to leave, the restaurant door opened and a couple entered.

The man, a burly figure in an expensive black coat and wearing a trilby immediately came over to Mathieu. The two shook hands and chatted briefly, but it wasn't until the man said, 'Mathieu who is your charming companion?' that Mathieu, reluctantly it seemed to Nanette, introduced her.

'Boris, this is my children's nanny. Netty, this is Boris, a business acquaintance.'

'Aw come now, Mathieu, more than a business acquaintance since last week. Remember how I help you with your little difficulty?'

Boris turned to Nanette, briefly acknowledged her with an abrupt *'Bonjour, mademoiselle'*, and turned his attention back to Mathieu.

Knowing the way society in Monaco worked Nanette was not surprised that once he'd learnt she was a mere nanny, Boris ignored her. As far as he was concerned she was just a servant and not important enough for him to bother with.

She wondered why Mathieu had introduced her as the nanny complete with the childish name the twins called her, when earlier he'd intimated he wanted them to get to know each other better. He must have realized he'd effectively precluded her from mixing with him and this particular business associate in the future.

Turning to take her coat from the waiter, Nanette had heard Boris say quietly, 'Tell Zac I need to talk to him urgently.'

Now, as she drank her coffee and watched the morning activity around her, she wondered what the connection between Zac and Boris was and how long Mathieu had known Boris.

The oft-quoted phrase about Monaco being 'a sunny place for shady people' came into her mind. What were Zac and Mathieu up to, doing business with a Russian whom she personally wouldn't trust an inch?

Thoughtfully, Nanette finished her coffee, left enough euros in the saucer to cover the bill and began to make her way down to the old port.

So much had changed since she lived here and yet some

things were still reassuringly familiar. From her bedroom balcony she'd struggled to remember the lines of the old port. To her eyes the new harbour extension, already crowded with the floating gin palaces belonging to the rich and famous, had blended in seamlessly.

Walking slowly along the quay, Nanette recognized some of the yachts, but to her relief there was no sign of *Pole Position* the boat Zac had treated himself to after winning the US Grand Prix in Indianapolis.

Knowing that he liked to have the yacht moored in Monaco and use it for parties both before and after the Grand Prix, Nanette knew that once *Pole Position* reappeared on its mooring, it wouldn't be long before Zac too was back in town.

Glancing up to the familiar skyline behind the Hotel de Paris as she walked up the hill, something jarred in her memory. It was a second or two before Nanette realized that the nineteenth-century villa where she'd had a tiny two-room apartment, had been replaced by a large ultra modern concrete building.

Shame; the old building had emitted a *belle époque* atmosphere of the Riviera in its heyday, which she'd loved. Zac though, had always complained about its lack of modern conveniences and had rarely visited her there.

His own large apartment had been in one of the ultramodern blocks a street or two away from Casino Square. Idly Nanette wondered if he still lived there or whether, like Mathieu, he had moved on to an even grander place. Whatever, she had no intention of walking anywhere near that particular area this morning.

Instead she took the Avenue Monte Carlo turning and strolled along, happily indulging in a spot of wishful window shopping in the expensive boutiques that lined the small street.

Dodging a string of excitable Japanese tourists, Nanette crossed the road and ran down a flight of steps into the Casino gardens. Last night Mathieu had mentioned an exhibition of sculpture being shown there by a little known Frenchwoman and she was looking forward to an hour or two wandering around the exhibits.

Sitting on the bed in her air-conditioned hotel bedroom, Vanessa pressed the 'save' key on Ralph's laptop before shutting the computer down and sliding it into the travel bag.

In a few minutes they would be on their way to the airport and the adventure would really begin. Their honeymoon had been wonderful, but now she was looking forward to spending the next few months with her new husband in one of the world's most exotic places. They would no longer be alone but part of a team. She hadn't yet met Harry and Nick, the cameramen, but Ralph had assured her they'd all get on. He'd worked with them both before.

'They're both passionate about the environment and I know they'll do all they possibly can to make sure the documentary shows the jungle as it is.'

Vanessa knew Ralph was determined his documentary was going to record the lives of the 'real' native Indians as they struggled to survive in a changing forest and it was one of the reasons he'd refused a sponsorship offer from a large multinational company.

'Staying independent, I can show the truth,' he'd said to Vanessa when he was outlining his plans. 'No-one can tell me what to film or say.'

Deciding she had time for one last shower before Ralph returned and they left for the airport, Vanessa quickly undressed and stepped under the warm water. Wrapping herself in the hotel's large bath towel afterwards, she crossed to the window and glanced out at the bustling street scene below.

Tomorrow this room would be a memory, and the chaotic scenes outside would have been replaced by forest and vegetation inhabited by strange sounding animals.

Their first few days in the Amazon jungle were going to be spent in the comfort of an 'eco tourist' camp before they and the crew moved off to explore more inaccessible areas with a native guide. Harry and Nick had flown up earlier with all their supplies and would have organized the next stage of the journey by the time she and Ralph arrived.

Vanessa turned to smile at Ralph as he closed the door behind him.

'Everything packed? Good' Ralph said. 'Ten minutes and we're off. Think I'll have a quick shower too. Might be sometime before we get the luxury of hot water again.'

Once they were both dressed, they picked up the backpacks Ralph had insisted were far more practical than suitcases in the jungle, and went to find their taxi for the trip out to the airport.

The office of the company that operated the small Cessna plane Ralph had chartered to fly them up to an outpost on the Amazon River, was situated at the edge of the airfield. Only internal flights operated from this rundown airstrip and walking towards the shabby hut where they had to check-in, Vanessa found herself worrying about the safety of the plane she was about to board.

'They do have regular maintenance and safety checks, don't they?' she asked Ralph.

'Of course. Don't worry. José and Carlos are very proud of their planes. Carlos told me they are the best in Brazil. Ah here's José,'

'Senhor Ralph and *a senhora*. We are ready for you. We go and—' The shrill ring of a telephone interrupted him and he glanced towards the desk. *'Bom-dia,'* he answered before immediately falling silent. When after several moments he replaced the receiver his eyes were bright with tears as he turned to face Ralph and Vanessa.

'That was another pilot telling me that a mutual friend has been shot down near Manaus.'

José swore angrily. 'The authorities apparently mistake it for a drug-running plane. The fools! But this time it is a *big* mistake – an American missionary and her family were on board. Now we shall have an investigation.'

Vanessa gazed at him horror struck. Manaus was a place on Ralph's itinerary. They were due to camp near there in a few weeks. She moved closer to Ralph, who placed a comforting arm around her shoulders.

'Do they often shoot planes out of the sky?' she asked.

José nodded vehemently. 'It happens,' he said shortly.

Vanessa shivered. Of course she'd known they were going into a drug-smuggling area, but she didn't do drugs, no-one she knew did drugs and she hadn't expected the drug trade to impinge on her life.

Images of the twins came into her mind. What if she and Ralph had been . . . *no!* She couldn't, wouldn't, follow that thought. Ralph had warned her about the dangers of this trip, from mosquitoes to alligators, but the shooting down of planes had never been mentioned.

Ralph glanced at José.

'I need to have a private word with my wife. Give us a couple of minutes, will you, please?'

José nodded. 'I'll wait by the plane. We need to take off in the next quarter of an hour so don't take too long for this private word.'

As José strolled off to prepare the plane, Ralph took Vanessa gently in his arms.

'Are you sure you want to go through with this? I know you're thinking about the consequences for the twins if we'd been on that plane. After this flight into the jungle, I promise our exploring will be done on foot, or by water. So, after today the next plane you get on will be the one taking us home.'

He gently kissed her on the forehead.

'But on the other hand, if you'd rather I continued on my own and you go home now, I'll understand.'

'Do you know what time we can expect Mathieu?' Jean-Claude asked, as he and Nanette sat on the terrace overlooking the swimming pool of his villa. 'If at all?'

'No,' Nanette said. 'I think he was hoping to be back before the twins went to bed tonight.'

'Has he said anything to you about his spot of recent trouble?' Jean-Claude asked.

Nanette shook her head. 'Seems to have blown over. He was worried that the authorities wouldn't let him leave but. . . .' She shrugged. 'That doesn't seem to have happened.'

'He refuses to talk to me about it at all,' Jean-Claude said, shaking his head. 'Just tells me not to worry. Everything has been sorted out. I just wish I knew what was going on.

Friends tell me he's mixing with some bad company.'

Nanette was silent, not knowing what to say.

The last time Mathieu had been home, he'd been in a very upbeat mood saying that life and business was good, but, like Jean-Claude, she was concerned about who he was doing business with. And what sort of business was he dealing in anyway?

'I'm a go between,' he said, when she'd casually asked him about his business before he left on this latest trip. 'A broker if you like. I find what people need, who's got it and put them together. I keep most of the info in my head so very little paperwork.'

And conveniently untraceable, Nanette couldn't help thinking.

Looking at Jean-Claude, Nanette asked, 'Do you know a man called Boris?'

'Only by reputation. I've never met him,' Jean-Claude said. 'Why?'

Nanette hesitated before answering.

'I think he was the business acquaintance who paid Mathieu's bail. He has some sort of connection with Zac, too.'

Before Jean-Claude could respond, his housekeeper appeared to say that lunch was ready.

'Five minutes, Anneke. We need to round up the twins,' Jean-Claude said.

The games room where Pierre and Olivia were playing a noisy game of table tennis was next to Jean-Claude's office. Nanette knew he ran a hugely successful corporate hospitality business, but she was amazed to see piles of papers and folders littering the desk and spilling on to the floor as she walked past. He obviously didn't follow his son's business philosophy of keeping paperwork to a minimum.

Jean-Claude saw her looking and said, 'My secretary left a few months ago and I haven't had a chance to find a replacement. Wouldn't have time to give me hand sorting things out, would you?'

'Of course,' Nanette said. 'I'd like to. Florence takes care of everything at the apartment and politely refuses all my offers of help. I'll come up tomorrow after I've taken the twins to school and make a start.'

'I also have another favour to ask,' Jean-Claude said. 'I have to go to a business cocktail party at the Hotel de Paris in the week and I need a partner. It's just a couple of hours. We could go for dinner somewhere afterwards if you like.'

Nanette hesitated, not sure she wanted to get involved in the Monte Carlo social scene again. But it was only a cocktail party, not the Red Cross Ball, one of the major social events of the season's calendar. And with over a month to go to the Monaco GP it was extremely unlikely that there would be anyone from the motor-racing world at the party.

She smiled at Jean-Claude. 'I'd love to come with you.'

'*Très bien*. Now let's have lunch.'

Nanette had forgotten it was the first European Grand Prix of the season that afternoon until Pierre mentioned it as they were eating dessert.

'Papa Jean-Claude, can I watch the San Marino Grand Prix please? Zac is on pole position.'

Olivia gave an exaggerated groan.

'Sure you can, and I'll keep you company for a while,' Jean-Claude said. 'But if you want to watch the introduction and driver interviews you'd better hurry up and finish your *crème bruleé*. The programme starts in five minutes,' he added, looking at his watch.

'Can I go swimming?' Olivia said. 'I don't want to watch the stupid race.'

'You can't go swimming straight after lunch. You'll have to wait for a bit,' Nanette said.

'That's OK. I'll read *The Lion, The Witch and The Wardrobe* until then.'

'How about you, Nanette? Are you going to watch the race with us?' Jean-Claude asked.

Nanette shook her head. It was years since she'd watched a Grand Prix, her interest in Formula 1 having hit an all time low when Zac had walked out on her. Silly really, when it was what had brought them together in the first place.

'No thanks. I'll go for a wander around the garden if that's all right,' she said. 'And then maybe I'll join Olivia in the pool.'

Strolling around the garden, Nanette found herself thinking about the race Zac had always called his home Grand Prix.

Although there were two more races before the Formula 1 circus arrived in town for the most glamorous race on the calendar, Monaco streets were already in the process of being barricaded into a race circuit. During the next few weeks the streets would be transformed with steel safety barriers and huge tiers of seating would appear around the racetrack.

Nanette knew that day-to-day living would become increasingly difficult as everything became geared to the smooth running of the biggest moneyspinner of the year. She also knew that the chances of her avoiding people from her past were slim.

She turned as Jean-Claude appeared on the terrace with

cups of coffee for them both.

'Thanks. How's the race going?'

'Usual procession,' Jean-Claude said. 'Need a few pit stops to start changing the order of cars and liven things up a bit.' He glanced at her. 'Nanette, I know it's none of my business, but are you going to cope with being in town for the Grand Prix? You know, better than most people I suspect, how invasive the whole Formula 1 thing is. The way it takes over completely. There'll be no escaping certain' – he paused – 'people.'

Nanette sipped her coffee as he continued, 'Vanessa tells me you have the nightmares. You also have no memory of what happened to you before the accident. Perhaps you should not be in town for the Grand Prix. If you want to stay up here with Olivia – or even go back to the UK for a few days – I can take care of Pierre if Mathieu happens to be away.' Jean-Claude regarded Nanette anxiously.

'Thank you,' Nanette said, 'but I think I have to stay.' She was silent for a few seconds before adding quietly, 'It's the third anniversary of my accident the week after the Grand Prix. Perhaps coming back to the scene of the crime will jerk my memory into action. Like the police doing reconstruction scenes in the hope of finding new witnesses.'

'Oh, I don't know, Nanette,' Jean-Claude said. 'But if you ever need a . . . I think you English call it a shoulder to cry on? Then I'm here.'

'Thank you,' she said gratefully. 'Olivia and I may well take you up on the offer of spending the actual race day up here though.'

Switching off her radio alarm Nanette lay in bed for a few

moments, thinking and planning the day ahead. Once she'd got the twins to school she was going shopping for a dress to wear to this evening's cocktail party and then she had an appointment at the hairdressers.

Knowing how immaculate the women who attended these parties always looked she knew she had to make an effort for Jean-Claude's sake. She didn't want to let him down with his business acquaintances.

Slipping her feet into her slippers, she stood up stretching her arms above her head as she did so, only to freeze in mid-action as she glanced out of the window.

Several yachts were about to enter the harbour and one of them looked uncomfortably familiar. Pulling her dressing-gown tight, Nanette stepped out on to her balcony and watched as the boats motored in.

The crew of *Pole Position* worked quickly and efficiently and it was only a matter of minutes before the yacht was secured on her mooring – directly opposite the block of apartments. Once the boat was tied up and the gangway lowered to the quay, Nanette held her breath waiting to see if Zac would appear.

But a lone crew member was the only person to run down and disappear along the embankment in the direction of the *supermarché*, reappearing minutes later with several baguettes and a bag of croissants for the crew's breakfast.

Thoughtfully Nanette ran the water for her bath, adding a generous amount of rose essence. With his yacht back in the harbour, it could only be a matter of time now before Zac, the Heel, appeared in Monaco. Fleetingly she wondered what his reaction to her being in town would be.

Stepping into the tub and sinking into the hot, scented

water, Nanette tried to drown out all thoughts of the past and Zac from her mind. Just because his yacht was here didn't mean he was likely to turn up tonight.

'Mmm, you smell nice,' Olivia said, when Nanette entered the sitting-room that evening. 'And your dress is cool.'

'Thank you. I hope it's the sort of thing people wear to cocktail parties. I'm a bit out of touch these days,' she said, glancing anxiously at Jean-Claude for reassurance.

'You look fine,' Jean-Claude said. 'The taxi is waiting, so shall we go? Is Mathieu home for the twins?'

Nanette shook her head.

'No. He rang earlier to say it will be late tonight before he gets back. Florence is here. I'll just tell her we're leaving.'

Early evening traffic was heavy and the taxi crawled up the hill towards Place du Casino.

'You're very quiet,' Jean-Claude said glancing at her. 'Are you OK?'

'I'm fine. Just a bit nervous. Haven't done much socializing recently.'

'Don't worry. *Pole Position* may be back on its mooring, but I happen to know Zac Ewart isn't in town,' Jean-Claude said quietly.

Nanette looked at him, surprised.

'When I saw the yacht this morning, I knew you'd be worried, so I made enquiries. Zac is busy testing in Jerez with his team for the next two days.'

'Oh, JC, thank you for that,' Nanette said gratefully, feeling the tension drain from her body. 'Now I can relax and help you with whatever you want me to do. Do you hope to promote your business tonight? Or is it a case of other businesses wanting you to use them. . . ? What's the matter?'

she asked anxiously, as Jean-Claude stared at her.

'My late wife was the only person who ever called me JC,' Jean-Claude said slowly.

'I'm sorry. I didn't mean to upset you. It sort of slipped out,' Nanette said. 'I'll stick to your full name in future.'

'No. It's fine. It was just the shock of hearing you say it. Please, I'd like you to call me JC, only perhaps not in front of my business associates tonight,' he said, smiling at her.

As the taxi drew up in front of the Hotel de Paris, the uniformed commissioner opened the door and ushered them up the steps into the opulent foyer with its chandeliers, deep carpets, marble stairs and enough fresh flowers to stock a florist's shop.

Once inside, where the head commissioner greeted Jean-Claude personally, they made their way to the Salon Berlioz, already buzzing with people.

Accepting glasses of champagne from an attentive waitress, Jean-Claude said, 'Right. Better start mixing. Let's start by talking to Robert, one of the wine merchants I use.'

For the next hour Jean-Claude circulated, introducing Nanette to so many people she forgot their names instantly. There was only one person with whom she had any sort of rapport and that was Evie, personal assistant to Luc, a formidable bear-like man who, Evie assured her, 'is a real sweetie.'

'Been in Monte long?' Evie asked, taking a smoked-salmon blini from a passing waiter and gesturing to Nanette to do the same.

'Just a few weeks,' Nanette said non-committally. 'You?'

'Six months. I love it. It's all so glamorous. I can't wait for the Grand Prix.'

Nanette smiled at her infectious enthusiasm, recognizing and remembering similar feelings when she'd first arrived.

'Are you Jean-Claude's assistant?'

'Sort of. Officially I'm his grandchildren's nanny.'

'Really? Gosh he doesn't look old enough to have grandkids,' Evie said, looking across at Jean-Claude who was saying an animated goodbye to Luc.

'Fancy meeting up for a coffee sometime?' Nanette said impulsively. 'I'm quite missing my girlfriends from back home and could do with some girly chat.'

'Love to,' Evie said. 'Take my card and give me a ring next week. Better go, I think Luc wants me. *Ciao.*'

'*Ciao,*' Nanette answered smiling.

She was still smiling when Jean-Claude joined her a couple of minutes later.

'Shall we go? I booked a table for eight o'clock at my favourite fish restaurant on Boulevard Grande Bretagne.' He stopped suddenly and looked at her anxiously. You do like fish, don't you? I didn't think to ask!'

'Yes, JC, I do,' Nanette laughingly reassured him.

A crowd of paparazzi had gathered on the pavement outside the hotel and flashbulbs started to pop as they walked past. Nanette, glancing briefly across to see if she recognized the blonde celebrity posing in the Casino entrance, thought 'rather her than me' and failed to notice a lone photographer moving backwards.

Jean-Claude's warning shout, 'Hey, mind where you're going,' and his attempt to pull her out of the way, was too late. The man collided with her heavily and they both fell over the small hedge that separated the pavement from the parkland grass in the middle of the Place du Casino.

Dazed, Nanette sat on the ground taking deep breaths for several moments and trying in vain to ignore the cameras that were now aimed in her direction.

'Are you all right?' asked a concerned Jean-Claude. 'Do you think you've broken anything?'

Nanette shook her head. 'I'll be fine. I'm just winded. But I could do with a hand to get up.'

Gently Jean-Claude helped her to her feet.

'*Mademoiselle*, I am so sorry,' the photographer said.

'It's OK.' Nanette said. 'I wasn't looking where I was going either.'

She looked at Jean-Claude. 'Could we just get to the restaurant please? I'd like some water.'

'Hey!' the photographer said suddenly. 'I recognize you. Aren't you the woman who nearly killed Zac Ewart?'

CHAPTER THREE

Days later, the words 'Aren't you the woman who nearly killed Zac Ewart?' were still ringing in Nanette's head as she kept going over and over the incident.

She'd known it was inevitable that someone from the past would recognize her, but somehow she'd expected it to happen during Grand Prix week when people she'd worked with years ago would be in town.

As she'd stared at the photographer, shocked into silence by his words, Jean-Claude had stopped a passing taxi, helped her into it and taken her back to his villa. He had comforted her, telling her that it was an isolated incident.

'You might have a certain notoriety for a few days now the press have realized you're back. Especially' – he hesitated before continuing – 'when Zac Ewart arrives. But I promise you it will pass.'

He had poured her a small brandy, encouraging her to sip it, while he phoned the restaurant and cancelled his reservation. He'd then cooked them pasta for supper before driving her back to the apartment.

Mathieu had been in when they arrived and Jean-Claude had quickly told him about the evening's incident before wishing Nanette 'Goodnight.'

As Mathieu saw JC out, Nanette opened the patio doors and stepped on to the balcony. Standing there watching the lights and looking over the harbour she was deep in thought when Mathieu joined her.

'I see *Pole Position* is back,' he said, looking down towards the yachts. There was a pause before he added, 'Zac is planning a big party on board in a couple of weeks I understand.'

'Of course he is,' Nanette said shortly, remembering when she'd done the organizing for on-board parties. 'And, knowing Zac, he won't stop at the one.'

Mathieu looked at her. 'Are you all right?' he asked gently.

Nanette nodded. 'Yes. Sorry, I didn't mean to snap. It's just that photographer tonight. . . .' She sighed, shook her head and didn't finish the sentence.

'Don't let it worry you,' Mathieu said. 'A couple more weeks, there will be so many famous people in town the paparazzi will forget about you.'

'Hope you're right,' Nanette answered. She looked at him hesitantly before asking, 'Are you in touch with Zac?'

Mathieu nodded. 'He's getting some pit lane passes for me.'

'Does he know I'm here?'

'Yes. I told him you were coming to look after the twins for me.'

'How did he react?'

Mathieu shrugged. 'He didn't say anything so I can't tell you.'

Mathieu was the first to speak again after a short silence.

'Talking of parties. We've got the Vintage Grand Prix this

year the weekend before the main one and I'm giving a lunch on the Sunday. Just friends and a few business contacts.' He glanced at her. 'I hope you'll join us?'

'Thanks. What about the twins though? Pierre will be keen, but Olivia will find the whole thing totally boring.'

Mathieu smiled. 'Maybe when she hears a certain pop star is on the guest list she'll come round.'

'Of course, you're directly above the start line here,' Nanette said, leaning on the balcony watching the cars moving along the Boulevard Albert 1st below. 'You'll have a great view. People will be begging to come.'

'The sound effects will be pretty awesome too,' Mathieu said. 'Nanette, I meant what I said the other evening about us getting to know each other better – I'm aiming to be home more in the next few weeks so I hope we can spend some time together. I'm sorry I had to cancel our date to see the tennis, but I hope you won't hold that against me.'

'Of course not. I was busy helping Jean-Claude sort out his office anyway.'

'I've promised the twins I'll take them out next Monday as it's a fête. I've got some friends who have a place up in the country near Grasse who've invited us for the day. Olivia and Pierre love it up there. Will you come, too?'

Before Nanette could reply his mobile rang and, with an apologetic smile, Mathieu turned from her and answered it. Nanette closed the balcony doors, mouthed 'goodnight' to a distracted Mathieu and went to bed with her thoughts.

A dishevelled Mathieu appeared the next morning as Nanette was getting the twins ready to leave for school.

'Morning,' he said, helping himself to a cup of coffee and

joining the twins as they ate their *pains au chocolat* at the breakfast bar in the kitchen.

'I've got to go away again this morning for a couple of days,' he said to the twins.

'What about our day out to Grasse?' Pierre demanded. 'You promised you'd take us. We're not going to have to cancel again are we?'

'Definitely not,' Mathieu said. 'I'll be back for that, and the good news is that Nanette is coming with us.'

'Mathieu, I've been thinking about that and I need to talk to you about it,' Nanette said.

Mathieu glanced at her. 'Talk later. Right now there are one or two papers I need to find for my trip and you two had better get a move on or you'll be late for school.' And Mathieu disappeared into the sitting-room. Seconds later he could be heard talking on his phone.

Nanette stifled a sigh. 'Come on you two. Dad's right. Let's go.'

Once she'd walked the twins to school and seen them into the grounds, Nanette hurried back to the apartment, hoping that Mathieu would still be there.

Because Nanette now had the bedroom Mathieu would normally have used as his office, he'd moved his computer, desk and a two-drawer filing cabinet into a tiny windowless area at the back of the sitting-room that housed a small fridge and a drinks cabinet for when he was entertaining guests on the balcony.

Florence was busy vacuuming as Nanette let herself into the apartment. She walked straight through the sitting-room, surprising Mathieu who was watching his printer waiting for the last piece of paper to join a freshly printed batch whilst mumbling into his phone. He jumped visibly at the sound of Nanette's voice and hurriedly switched the phone off before turning to face her.

'Mathieu about the trip to Grasse. Is it the de Oliviers' farm you're visiting?'

'Yes.'

'In that case I'd rather not go with you.'

'Why on earth not?'

Nanette looked at him quizzically. 'Why do you think? Zac and I used to visit them regularly when they lived up at Eze. I'm pretty sure they—'

'Would be very pleased to see you again,' Mathieu interrupted.

Nanette shook her head. 'I'd still rather not go.'

Mathieu looked at her before saying stonily, 'You are here to look after the twins. It's not really for you to decide whether you go or not. I could insist you accompany us.'

'I do look after the twins – when they are not at school I organize their lives,' Nanette said, taking a deep breath. 'I've actually seen more of them than you have in the last few weeks – you're always dashing off somewhere or other. You certainly weren't around for Pierre's after school football match, or Olivia's music exam,' she added crossly. 'Olivia has already told me how much they are both looking forward to having you to themselves on Monday.' She paused, before adding slowly, 'But, Mathieu, if you don't think I'm doing enough for the twins, you can always tell me to go and take over the job yourself. I'd be quite happy to go home – I didn't want to come back here in the first place!'

She looked him straight in the eyes before adding, 'I'm not sure how Vanessa would react to you sacking me though.'

*

That first night in the eco-tourism camp, Vanessa struggled to sleep under the mosquito net in the hammock slung between two beams of the traditional native hut, reliving the last few hours over and over in her mind.

As Ralph had held her in his arms after José had told them about the plane being shot down, saying she could go home to the twins if she wanted, she'd longed in her heart to do just that. But knowing how important this expedition and her presence on it was to Ralph, she'd steeled herself to continue.

Praying that Ralph was right when he assured her, it was extremely unlikely that another innocent plane would be shot out of the sky in the near future, 'Lessons will have been learnt', were his words, she'd taken a deep breath and climbed into the small plane.

To her surprise once they were airborne she'd relaxed and enjoyed the long flight. José had flown them over volcanoes, rivers and acres and acres of jungle. Ralph, quickly realizing he was extremely knowledgeable about his country, had spent most of the journey quizzing him about life in the jungle.

From her vantage point in the small plane the green jungle canopy below had looked to Vanessa like nothing more than giant knobbly heads of broccoli allowed to grow and grow.

Eventually José had landed on a dirt runway that appeared to be in the middle of a native village. As the door of the plane opened and she'd stepped out, the heat and the humidity had enveloped her completely. Seeing her discomfort, José immediately summoned one of the native women who had clustered around, to take her to the shelter of a small hut and give her a cool drink.

After watching José take off safely for his return journey, Ralph joined Vanessa in the hut. 'Ready for the next part?' he asked. 'The boat is waiting.' And, taking her by the hand, he helped her down a long length of rickety wooden steps to a small quay where a large motorized wooden canoe was moored.

Once on board, a canopy almost the length of the boat shielded the passengers from the intense heat and, as the canoe began to chug through the water, Vanessa appreciated the light breeze that fanned her face. As they made their way upriver, the noise of the boat's engine mingled with the squawking of a large flock of parakeets. With the summer rainy season well under way, the river was high and much of the surrounding lowland was flooded.

'Look,' Ralph said, laughing, as he pointed to a log floating downstream. It took Vanessa a couple of seconds before she too saw the family of turtles hitching a lift on the water-sodden trunk. Gazing out across the wide expanse of water Vanessa tried to see the way ahead but the river appeared to snake its way forever through lush jungle, giving no hint of what lay beyond.

The river journey took over two hours and by the time they reached the camp where they were due to spend a couple of days acclimatizing themselves to their surroundings, Vanessa's clothes were damp and sticking uncomfortably to her body. The canoe tied up alongside a small quay and suddenly native Indians were all around, helping them land and then to negotiate a bridged wooden walkway that led to the village.

Built by the natives using traditional materials and techniques, there were several thatched wooden structures of various sizes, all on stilts, all giving the appearance of an authentic and indigenous rainforest village. It was only when she saw the western touches that had been added in the form of private bathrooms with sun-heated showers to the guest cabins that Vanessa realized the place was purpose built for the tourists.

Exhausted, Vanessa climbed up into the hut allocated to her and Ralph, determined to at least shower and change her clothes before joining the others for a meal. Served in the communal dining-room they made the acquaintance of the other guests who were amazed to learn of Ralph's plans to take his new wife on a trek through unchartered, inhospitable jungle.

As they tucked into a hearty local soup followed by fish baked in vine leaves, Vanessa heard one earnest man tell Ralph quietly, 'Remember, all the money in the world, won't get you out of the jungle in a hurry.'

Making their way back to their hut at the end of the evening, Vanessa had asked Ralph what the man was warning him about.

'Usual stuff about drug barons and gold smugglers.' Ralph shrugged. 'He didn't seem to grasp the fact that my interest is in what remains of the ecological system, not the people who have ruined it. I have no intention of crossing swords with the local bandits.'

Vanessa shifted in her hammock trying to shut out the jungle's night-time noises of howler monkeys and raucous insects. Briefly she wondered what other animals were out there, unheard, going about their nocturnal lives close to the encampment.

She shivered apprehensively. In twenty-four hours she wouldn't even have the comfort of a native hut between her and the jungle inhabitants.

Ralph had decided to bring their departure from the camp forward by a day.

'Harry and Nick have everything organized, so no point in hanging around in this pseudo environment,' he'd said disparagingly, waving his hand around the campsite. 'I know it is helping to remedy years of destruction to the jungle, but I want to get to where the real jungle is. See some natives living in the traditional way.'

Tomorrow they would leave the comforts of the camp behind them and then 'Our adventure really will begin,' Ralph had said excitedly, as they'd kissed each other goodnight.

'You sure you won't change your mind and come with us?' Mathieu asked, as he and the twins left for their day out in the country. The outing hadn't been mentioned since their argument a few days before and Nanette was relieved that Mathieu had allowed the subject to drop. This morning he seemed to have forgotten his earlier accusations and was happy to be going with the twins on his own after all.

'It will be quiet here on your own all day.'

Nanette shook her head. 'Quite sure, thanks. Besides, I won't be on my own all day – I'm meeting Jean-Claude later. Enjoy yourselves.'

She was just closing the door behind them when Mathieu called out, 'Nanette, there's a package for you in my office. I'm sorry I forgot to tell you yesterday when it came. It's on my desk.'

Nanette recognized Patsy's handwriting on the large envelope. Taking a paperknife out of the desk tidy she carefully slit open the envelope. Replacing the paperknife, a crumpled piece of paper beside the wastepaper basket caught her attention. Picking it up she saw it was a detailed map of the Amazon clearly torn out of an atlas.

The twins were following Vanessa's progress so there was nothing unusual in Mathieu having a map of the trip – in fact there was a large-scale one pinned to the wall – but this one had some of its place names circled in red and haphazardly linked together with numbers written against them. Puzzled, Nanette tried to work out what they could possibly represent, before deciding that it was probably a piece of scrap paper that Mathieu had been doodling on and threw it into the wastepaper basket where Mathieu had obviously intended it to go.

Going to her own room, Nanette carefully pulled out the contents of the envelope. A long, newsy letter from Patsy was wrapped around another sealed brown official envelope. Pensively, Nanette placed the envelope in the drawer of her dressing-table. Even without opening it she knew exactly what it contained. Taking Patsy's letter with her she went to make a cup of coffee.

Because it was a fête day, Florence had the day off and for the first time since she'd arrived Nanette was completely alone in the apartment. Coffee cup in hand she wandered around enjoying the solitude. Pausing outside Mathieu's closed bedroom door she realized she'd only ever had glimpses of that particular room – the door was always closed. Curiously, and smothering her guilty feelings, Nanette turned the handle, only to find the door was locked.

Nanette mused, sipping her coffee, was Mathieu just keen on privacy, or did he have something to hide in there? Deep in thought, she returned to Mathieu's temporary office. The computer was switched off. The desk, aside from the desk tidy was empty. Not even a diary. And the filing cabinet was locked. The only discordant thing in the room was the crumpled atlas page in the wastepaper basket. She retrieved it and, smoothing it out, wandered back into the sitting-room. Maybe it was only a piece of waste paper, but somehow she had a feeling it was more than that. Perhaps she'd show it to Jean-Claude later and see if he had any ideas.

Standing by the sitting-room window she glanced out at the harbour and froze as she saw a figure sitting at a table on the stern deck of *Pole Position*. Even from her viewpoint, nine floors up she had no difficulty in recognizing Zac. Or the man he was now standing up to welcome on board – Boris.

Hoping she was shielded from view by the lemon tree in its pot on the balcony, Nanette watched as the two men were served coffee by a stewardess before Boris handed Zac what looked like a large packet.

Ten minutes later, both men stood up, shook hands and Boris took his leave of Zac, making his way slowly along the gangway back to a large black car waiting for him on the harbour road.

On board *Pole Position* Nanette could see Zac punching a number into his mobile phone before holding it up to his ear, and moving his head so that it was obvious he was looking directly up at the apartment. Nanette stepped slowly away from the window. Had he seen her after all? Realized she'd been watching him and Boris?

The unexpected shrill buzz of the apartment doorbell made

her jump and she hurried to open it.

'*Bonjour, Nanette.* Happy May Day.' Jean-Claude lightly kissed her on both cheeks before handing her a pot of Lilies of the Valley.

'Thank you, JC,' Nanette said, surprised. She'd forgotten all about the tradition of giving the highly scented flowers on 1 May as a sign of friendship – and love.

'You look a little flustered,' Jean-Claude said, looking at her anxiously. 'Nothing wrong is there?'

'Zac is in town. I've just been watching him and his friend Boris meeting on *Pole Position*,' she explained.

'Is this Boris still there? I would be interested in seeing what he looks like,' Jean-Claude said, walking out on to the balcony quickly.

'No. He left a few minutes ago. But Zac is still on board.'

Joining him out on the balcony, Nanette could see Zac now in the cockpit gesticulating at one of his crew. As they watched, Zac turned and glanced upwards, raising his hand in greeting as he saw Jean-Claude. Rather than acknowledge him, Nanette turned and went back into the sitting-room.

'I thought we'd have lunch at the Automobile Club,' Jean-Claude said. 'Or anywhere you like,' he added quickly, seeing the look on her face.

'It's just that Zac's in town,' Nanette apologized. 'I know it's his favourite place for lunch. And I'm not quite ready to meet him socially yet. Could we go somewhere else please?'

'Why don't we walk up to Saint Nicholas Square?' Jean-Claude said. 'It's a bit touristy, but on the plus side I doubt that Zac will venture up that way on a fête day.'

Nanette looked at him gratefully. 'I'll just get my bag.'

*

To Nanette's relief, and by mutual unspoken agreement, they left the apartment block by the quieter exit on to a back street so she didn't have to walk past *Pole Position*.

The weather for the May Day holiday was perfect – blue sky, a gentle breeze and warm sunshine. Joining the throngs of tourists they began making their way up towards the Palace.

Saint Nicholas Square was in the labyrinth of busy narrow streets that clustered around the cathedral in the old town. Choosing an outside table at one of the restaurants, they sat down under a gaily stripped umbrella. Snatched conversations in French, English, Italian and the inevitable Japanese floated in the air around them. An attentive waiter handed them a menu.

'*Vous faites décider . . . ah, pardon* Nanette. I forgot. I will speak English.' Jean-Claude said. 'Have you decided what you'd like to eat?'

'JC, please speak in French,' Nanette answered. 'Not using it for three years mine's a bit rusty, but I do still understand. I need to start speaking it again too.'

She glanced at the menu. 'I think I'll have the *plat du jour, s'il vous plait.*'

Sipping her glass of ice-cold rosé Nanette looked at Jean-Claude.

'Something else I haven't used for three years arrived today,' she said quietly.

Jean-Claude looked at her in puzzlement.

Nanette pictured the envelope in the drawer before saying quietly, 'My driving licence has been returned. My driving ban is finished.'

'But that is good, isn't it?' Jean-Claude said. 'Now you can truly put the past behind you and start driving again.'

'I'm not sure that I have the confidence to get behind the wheel of a car again.'

'If you are nervous I can come with you for the first few times,' Jean-Claude offered.

'I don't know that it's that simple, JC.' Nanette fiddled with her cutlery. 'What if—?'

Jean-Claude stopped her in mid sentence.

'*Non*. No *what ifs* Nanette. You've been punished for the accident. Now you must put it behind you and get on with your life. I forbid you to let it blight the future.'

In spite of herself Nanette smiled at the stern look on Jean-Claude's face.

'I know you're right, but I don't have a car at the moment anyway, so' – she shrugged – 'I shall avoid the issue for at least a few more weeks.'

After an exasperated 'Tch' Jean-Claude changed the subject.

'I hope Mathieu has invited you to the lunch he's hosting Vintage Grand Prix weekend?'

'Yes, I'm looking forward to it. Will you be there?'

'Yes and no. I've been persuaded to get my Lotus out of mothballs and give it an outing, so I shall be spending most of my Sunday with the mechanics. Be interesting to drive on a circuit again after so long. Especially this one.'

'I didn't know you'd been a racing driver,' Nanette said.

'Only very briefly. It was at the time the sport was changing rapidly into big business with the manufacturers taking over. It simply became too expensive without a sponsor; I found myself priced out of the market.' He shrugged. 'And if I'm honest I lacked the competitive edge that people like Mansell and Senna had. So, the car has been under wraps for the last few years. I've got the next couple of weeks to finish checking it over mechanically and prepare it. Of course, I don't expect to be placed, but must admit I'm looking forward to the weekend.'

'Who have you got supporting you on the day?' Nanette asked. 'You'll need someone in the pits to help.'

'Not a problem. There are always young lads wanting to get involved and I've got a mechanic called David coming over from Le Cannet to help. He used to work the circuit so he knows the ropes.'

He glanced at her. 'And Zac has offered me the expertise of one of his mechanics if I need it. The Formula One circus will be arriving in town by then with only a week to go to the Grand Prix proper. Looks as though it might be Zac's year,' he added casually. 'I see he's leading the championship and is favourite to win next week in Germany.'

Nanette nodded. Despite herself she'd been keeping an eye on the results since the drivers had arrived back in Europe from Australia.

'My offer still stands by the way,' Jean-Claude said. 'You're more than welcome to use the villa as a hideaway anytime – not just on race day. After the Spanish race Zac is certain to be in town more or less permanently until the Grand Prix.'

'I know,' Nanette said diffidently, remembering previous years when Zac had used the run up to the Monaco Grand Prix to do a lot of socializing. She sighed inwardly. The inevitable meeting was getting closer.

'You will have to meet him face to face one day, Nanette. What will you do then?' Jean-Claude asked gently.

Nanette shook her head before saying slowly, 'I don't know.'

*

For the next couple of weeks Monaco continued to gear itself up for the busiest part of its year. The needs of the vintage Grand Prix weekend complicated things as everything had to be ready a week earlier, which had added a manic frenzy to the normal busy preparations.

Walking to school every day, Nanette and the twins got used to dodging around obstacles on the pavement, lorries parked unloading yet more essential street furniture and the inevitable crowds of tourists being disembarked into the Principality for the day from the cruise ships moored in the harbour.

Every street had an army of workmen busy hammering and fixing things into place. Terraces of stands had taken over the hillside and the harbour, large television screens had appeared in strategic places around the route and the barriers were in place around the length of the circuit. Fresh white paint detailed the starting grid below Nanette's balcony.

The main players in the Formula 1 circus had yet to arrive, but the supporting sideshow of trucks, traders and hangers-on, were already making their presence felt. The harbour was jam-packed with more and more luxury yachts whose owners were all determined to be a part of the glamorous scene.

Nanette had so far managed to avoid walking directly past *Pole Position* but this morning returning from taking the twins to school, she had no choice but to walk along that side of the embankment, as the other side had been blocked. Looking straight ahead she walked quickly, not looking at the boats until she was certain she had left *Pole Position* well behind.

With a deep breath of relief, she managed to cross the road

and make her way into the small supermarché. Mathieu had asked her to pick up some croissants for his breakfast on her way back.

'Florence won't be in this morning – dentist or something,' Mathieu had said.

Resisting the urge to buy herself a *pomme de tart* for her own breakfast, Nanette held the still warm croissants carefully as she let herself into the quiet apartment. She switched on the coffee machine before laying a tray with cups and plates and the croissants.

'Hi Mathieu. I'm back,' she called. 'Do you want your croissants and coffee on the balcony?'

The words died in her throat as a familiar figure appeared in the kitchen doorway.

'The balcony sounds fine. Hello, Nanette.' As Nanette stood in total shock looking at him, Zac Ewart walked purposefully into the kitchen – and back into her life.

CHAPTER FOUR

Dressed in his favoured black jeans and polo shirt, a suede jacket slung casually over his shoulders, sunglasses perched on top of his head, Zac regarded Nanette contemplatively, his eyes taking in everything about her appearance.

Nanette, frozen into stillness, managed a strangled, 'Hello Zac.'

'That's not much of a greeting for an old friend,' and Zac moved forward to kiss her cheek.

'Don't you dare,' Nanette said, between clenched teeth.

Zac stepped back, his hands in the air. 'Sorry.'

'How did you get in here anyway?'

'Mathieu let me in – and then remembered he had an urgent appointment in Fontvielle.' Zac gazed at her serenely. 'So, we have the place to ourselves. We can catch up with all our news over breakfast.' He picked up the breakfast tray. 'I think we agreed on the balcony?'

Nanette, knowing full well there was no urgent appointment for Mathieu, followed Zac slowly out to the balcony.

'How are you?' Zac asked, as he placed the tray on the table.

'How am I? Why should you care? It's been three years –
three years, Zac – since the accident, without a word from
you. Why the sudden interest?'

'I was glad to hear you were back. I care about you – I've
missed you.'

Nanette gazed at him in disbelief.

'If you missed me that much, why didn't you get in touch?
Visit me in England? And,' Nanette took a deep breath, 'I
thought you more than *cared* for me – we were engaged. I
thought you loved me. Disappearing out of my life without
even officially breaking off our engagement was cruel, Zac.'

Zac regarded her steadily. 'I'm sorry, Nanette. It seemed the
right thing to do at the time.'

'Right for whom?'

'Me. Selfish, I know but there it is,' and he shrugged his
shoulders apologetically.

Nanette turned away and leant on the balcony rail, her
senses in disarray. She'd spent a lot of time with this man, had
thought she was going to spend the rest of her life with him,
but their three years apart had turned him into a stranger, and
she didn't know what to say to him.

'Coffee?' Zac handed her a cup. 'Has Mathieu told you
about my party next week? I hope you're coming.'

Nanette shook her head, but before she could say anything
Zac continued, 'I'd at least feel you were starting to forgive
and forget the past, and my running out on you, if you'd
come.'

'I don't know that I do forgive you,' Nanette said sharply.
'As for forgetting, well, my memory is still hazy about the
actual accident, but I doubt that I'll ever forget its
consequences, or the hell of the last three years.'

Zac, Nanette noted, had the grace to look upset at her outburst.

'You still don't remember any details of the accident then?' he asked, stirring his coffee, not looking at her.

'No. Other than it was only the second time I'd driven the car,' Nanette said.

She didn't tell him, she remembered vividly all the details of the afternoon when Zac had presented her with the racy convertible – an early birthday present. She'd loved it and had immediately jumped into it and driven Zac around Monaco, showing the car off to all her friends.

Nine hours later the car was a mangled wreck on the auto-route and she was in intensive care in the Princess Grace Hospital.

Nanette stared at him.

'And no-one has ever explained why I was flown back to the UK within forty-eight hours of coming out of intensive care. Why wasn't I just allowed to stay here and recover?'

'Everyone thought you'd be better off at home,' he said evasively.

'This was my home. And who's this *everyone?*' Nanette demanded.

There was a brief silence as Zac pulled his croissant apart before turning to face her.

'It was my decision,' he said quietly. 'I made all the arrangements.'

'Didn't want the responsibility of caring for me, is that it? Scared I was going to be permanently scarred or disabled?'

Zac shook his head. 'I just thought you'd be better off where Patsy could administer some tender loving care. Nurse you back to health. Come on, Nanette, you know what my racing schedule is like from June to October, I'm never in town for more than two or three days at a time. There was no way I could play doctors and nurses all summer.'

'But why—'

Zac held up his hands. 'Stop. Enough questions. All I can say is, I'm sorry I hurt you in the past, but as far as I'm concerned, it's history. I'm glad you're back in Monaco looking so well and I hope we can be friends.'

As he said this, he looked at her quizzically before adding, 'Or at the very least be civil to each other when we meet.'

When she didn't answer, he sighed before reaching into the inside pocket of his jacket and taking out a brown envelope.

'Pit lane passes. If I don't see you before, I'll see you on Sunday – and please think about coming to my party. *Pole Position* has been refurbished recently – she's looking really smart, I'd like you to see the changes. Right, thanks for breakfast— Stay there. I'll see myself out. Ciao.'

As the apartment door slammed behind him, Nanette sank down trembling on to a chair, relief flooding through her body. The meeting she'd been dreading was over and she could only be grateful that it had taken place privately, not in public. At least now that it had happened she wouldn't have to skulk around Monaco worrying she was about to bump into him and wondering what his reaction would be. He was right, of course, they were bound to meet up from time to time and it was far better all round if they were civil to each other.

Not that she felt very civil towards him right now, after that casual remark about forgiving and forgetting the past. As if it was that easy. He still hadn't explained why he had not been in touch once he'd shipped her back to Patsy.

Sitting there, trying to analyse her feelings about the meeting and for Zac Ewart, Nanette frowned. There were still questions to which she needed answers and until her memory returned fully, Zac Ewart was the only person who could give them, which clearly he had no intention of doing.

Smothering a sigh, she picked up the breakfast tray and returned it to the kitchen. For how much longer was the legacy of her past to haunt her future?

After Nanette had collected the twins from school on Wednesday afternoon they walked up to Jean-Claude's villa where Mathieu had said he would join them in the swimming pool.

There was no sign of anyone when they arrived, but Nanette could hear raised voices coming from Jean-Claude's study.

'You two go on down to the pool room and get changed but do not get into the pool until I, or Daddy, get there. Understand? I'll just go and tell Papa Jean-Claude we're here and see where your father is.'

Nanette recognized Mathieu's angry voice as she got close to the window of the ground-floor study.

'Get off my back, Papa. I know what I'm doing and I don't need your advice.'

'The last time you shouted that at me you ended up needing me though – and my money, remember?'

'Never going to let me forget that, are you? I was nineteen for god's sake!'

'Whether you want my advice or not, I'm telling you you're getting involved in dangerous waters. These people you're involved with will cast you aside when they have no further use for you. They'll throw you to the lions without a second thought.'

'I don't happen to agree with you, but if it happens – it's my problem not yours.'

'The fact that you're my son and you're besmirching the family name makes it my problem.'

Nanette could hear the tension in Jean-Claude's voice as she edged nearer the study door.

'Just remember the twins too. They need their father around. Not languishing in jail for some unrealistic get-rich-quick crime he was stupid enough to get involved with. And, Mathieu, never forget, you can be thrown out of the Principality. If the Grimaldis can do it to one of their own, then it can happen to anyone.'

To Nanette's ears, the silence following Jean-Claude's last remark seemed to last forever. She was just about to knock on the door and call out, when Mathieu spoke again. This time he appeared to be measuring his words carefully.

'Papa, please trust me on this. I do actually know what I'm doing and in a couple of months you, and everyone else, will realize it too.'

'I hope so, Mathieu. I sincerely hope so,' Jean-Claude said quietly.

Both men turned as Nanette opened the study door.

'Hi. The twins are waiting for you down by the pool, Mathieu,' she said.

'Sorry – I forgot the time. I'll see you later, Dad,' and Mathieu left.

Jean-Claude looked at her. 'How much did you overhear?'

Nanette shrugged. 'Enough to realize how worried you still are about Mathieu. Has something else happened?'

'No – other than I have now met Boris and took an instant dislike to the man. Also' – he hesitated – 'there are rumours flying around about an illegal cartel involving several high-profile personalities.'

'But you don't know for sure that Mathieu is involved in that?'

Jean-Claude shook his head. 'No. But I have reason to believe Zac Ewart is – and, as you and I both know, he and Mathieu are very close.'

Vanessa stumbled over some exposed roots of an immense tree that towered above her as she followed their machete-wielding guide along the muddy track, taking them deeper and deeper into the forest.

All day they had hacked their way into the depths of the steamy, lush forest. Now their destination, a native village, was only an hour away.

Trudging in single file behind Ralph and the others, Vanessa felt both tired and exhilarated. The clean oxygen-filled air, heavy with moisture, had initially somehow bestowed a feeling of euphoria and excitement on her, but now her clothes were beginning to smell and feel damp from all the humidity.

Her skin was itching where unknown insects had bitten her. Her head was sweaty from the wide brimmed hat she was wearing to deflect the sun and to stop the legions of creepy crawlies above her in the rain forest's canopy, from falling into her hair. She longed for the day to end.

Their trek had taken them between columns of trees so tall their tops disappeared from view, with long liana vines hanging and wrapping themselves around the trunks. Vast spider-webs had spanned the green vegetation, where some leaves were as huge as the parasol Vanessa dreamily imagined sitting under and relaxing.

At ground level everything appeared to be in a state of flux. Strange smells wafted up from where plants were growing, decaying, dying, surrounded by lots of bugs, snakes and other things that Vanessa just knew were waiting to take a bite out of her.

As the day wore on, the sounds of the jungle had become familiar. Sloths shaking the treetops looking for a resting spot, the echoing cries of the howler monkeys as they swung through the trees and the ever-present noise of the cicadas mingling with birdsong became background noises to the group as they hacked their way through the rain forest.

The village clearing appeared unexpectedly. One minute the guide was leading them along a muddy track beneath the jungle canopy, the next they came to an abrupt standstill as their way was barred by a group of native Indians holding their hunting spears at arm's length.

For one heart-stopping moment, Vanessa thought they were about to be attacked, but it was simply the welcoming party come to escort them into the village.

The primitive palm thatched huts on their stilts stood around the edge of the clearing, where the village animals, including a fat pig and several roosters, were roaming freely scouring the land for scraps.

Walking to the centre of the encampment with curious villagers eyeing them from a distance, Vanessa noticed a small child standing close to her mother watching the strangers with wide brown eyes.

Vanessa smiled at her and was rewarded with a shy smile

in return before the little girl turned and ran after a baby pig, before settling down in the dust to stroke and play with it. Looking at her, naked and beautifully brown, with her bare feet planted firmly on the earth, the phrase 'being at one with nature' came into Vanessa's mind. This little girl was definitely in harmony with the natural world that she lived in.

Briefly Vanessa envied her the simplicity of her childhood – and her life to come.

The chief shaman came forward to welcome them and showed them to the hut reserved for visitors.

They'd barely had time to sling their hammocks between the beams and change their damp clothes before a young woman appeared inviting them to come and eat the special meal the villagers had prepared in their honour.

There were bowls of yucca soup, rice, fish, fruit and, to Vanessa's horror, large white live grubs and what was clearly organ meat from various animals, all laid out in their honour. She looked at Ralph in dismay.

'I don't want to upset anyone but I can't eat those things,' she whispered, pointing to the wriggling white grubs and the meat.

'Stick to the rice and fish,' Ralph advised quietly. 'And have some fruit.'

As Vanessa began to peel a banana a small monkey who had been wandering around scratching the earth, suddenly ran up to her, snatching the banana from her, before jumping on to her lap and settling down to eat it. Vanessa looked at him in amazement. She must remember to tell the twins about this.

Listening to fragments of the conversation around her as

she watched the monkey, Vanessa realized the village was struggling to survive.

Angela, the mother of the little girl Vanessa had seen earlier, was shaking her head sadly as she spoke to Ralph in fragmented Spanish.

'It is terrible with the forest – so much destruction. People need to find a way of surviving, of helping the jungle to grow back. Much is being done but the bandits, they still spoil things.' She shrugged her shoulders. 'The drugs and the gold smuggling is taking over our culture even here in this tiny village. We have a school now, but the children – what future do they have? The government want our people to report anyone who abuses the forest but we're not going to risk our lives, are we?'

Angela looked at Ralph in distress.

'How would my children survive if I ended up with a rifle in my mouth?'

Early on Sunday morning, pit lane passes hanging around their necks, Nanette and the twins crossed the Boulevard Albert 1st at a designated crossing place between the barriers, and made their way to the area where Jean-Claude was fine-tuning his Lotus before the race.

Pierre was excited at seeing all the old cars close up, but Olivia was already bored. Mathieu and Florence were busy preparing the apartment for the lunch party and had gently suggested Nanette took the twins out of the way. Olivia had protested saying she'd rather stay in her room, but Mathieu had insisted.

'Papa Jean-Claude's down there getting ready. Go and wish him good luck. He'd love to see you all,' and Mathieu had practically pushed them out of the apartment.

Along the pit lane the cars with their curiously old-fashioned looks were the star attractions. Pierre was fascinated to see a car that had raced in the very first Monaco Grand Prix over sixty years ago on display at the end of the pit lane enclosure.

And even Olivia was impressed when Jean-Claude told them how well his qualifying laps had gone.

'Can't believe the old girl went so well. Fourth on the grid. Just have to hope she keeps going now.' He patted the dark green bonnet of the car gently. 'Imagine I'm alongside Stirling on the third row,' he said, looking at Nanette.

Nanette smiled at his boyish enthusiasm. 'Good luck,' she said, leaving Jean-Claude and his mechanic to finish their adjustments to the car.

Strolling along the pit lane with the twins, Nanette remembered the countless times she'd been involved in preparations for Grand Prix races with Zac all over the world, but there was something different about this pit lane. It took her several minutes to realize exactly what it was.

There were crowds of people milling around and there was the usual frenzy of mechanics preparing cars for racing but it was all rather subdued and, like the cars, old-fashioned. The razzamatazz atmosphere of a modern Formula 1 grand prix was missing. Next week Monaco would be in the grip of twenty-first-century racing car fever as the modern Formula 1 road-show took over and Monaco turned itself into the most glamorous race-track in the world, but this Sunday morning, it was all about nostalgia.

Knowing that once the racing started they wouldn't be able to leave the pit lane, Nanette ushered the twins across the road and they made their way slowly home.

Back in the apartment, Pierre grabbed Mathieu's binoculars and took up his position on the balcony where he had a good view of both the starting grid and the pit lane exit. Guests were starting to arrive, at one of whom, a tall lanky teenager, Olivia took one look and gasped.

'Dad didn't say *he* was coming,' she said. Nanette laughed at the expression on her face.

'Who is he?'

Olivia looked at her in disbelief. 'You must recognize him. It's Foxey. He's the lead singer with a really, really cool band. Les Grenouille's.'

'Oh,' Nanette said, watching as Olivia ran to her room to change into her 'best' jeans – the ones with the tear in the knee – and to fetch her autograph book.

'Be really cool if he'd sign it for me,' she said. 'Do you think he will?'

'Don't see why not,' Nanette said.

Nanette was less than thrilled to see the next person who arrived – Boris. Accompanied by a group of six men and the blonde woman Nanette had seen with him in the restaurant, he walked confidently into the apartment. After a cursory glance in her direction and a polite *'Bonjour'*, he went through to join Mathieu.

Nanette stood undecided. She didn't fancy going out on to the balcony and making small talk to Boris and his cronies until other guests arrived. When the doorbell rang, she quickly called out to Florence, 'Don't worry, I'll get it,' and opened the door to find Evie and her boss, Luc, standing there.

Together they went through to the balcony where Mathieu

was supervising pre-lunch nibbles and drinks. Accepting a glass and taking an hors d'oeuvre Nanette and Evie edged their way along towards Pierre.

'It's Papa Jean-Claude's race next,' he said. 'Look here he comes out of the pits,' and he trained the binoculars down on the pit lane exit.

'Gosh, from up here they look like the Dinky toys my kid brother used to play with,' Evie said, leaning over to get a better look.

Several of the cars were already on the grid having driven around the circuit to get to their starting positions and their mechanics were once again thronging around giving them final checks in the last twenty minutes before the formation lap.

Nanette watched as Jean-Claude took his Lotus up the hill before disappearing from view along the part of the track that went past the Casino.

By the time he emerged from the tunnel and was negotiating the bends by the swimming pool, most of Mathieu's guests had arrived and the balcony was buzzing.

Nanette, looking out across the harbour, saw Zac on *Pole Position* and breathed a small sigh of relief. He was obviously not planning on joining them for lunch. Since the morning he'd come to the apartment expressing the desire that they should be civil to each other in public, Nanette had been wondering where and when their next encounter would be.

Evie saw her looking at the yachts.

'Is that *Pole Position*? I've been invited to a party on board tomorrow. Do you know Zac Ewart?'

Nanette smiled. Evie was exactly the kind of girl Zac liked to surround himself with. She nodded.

'Yes I've known Zac for years.'

She glanced at Evie as she said this. Evie, being new in town, clearly had no idea of her past relationship with Zac.

Nanette, knowing the way the grapevine worked, knew it wouldn't be long before someone told Evie all the gory details. She hesitated, perhaps she should get in first with her version – the details she could remember anyway.

'Oh great, you'll be going to the party then,' Evie said, and the opportunity was gone.

'Not sure,' Nanette said evasively.

A party on board the boat on which she had organized many a party in the past, full of people who had ostracized her after the accident wasn't a scenario she fancied. Could she really face it?

'It's about to start,' Pierre said excitedly. 'The lights are on.'

Watching the old cars take off, Nanette hoped Jean-Claude would do well – or at least finish the race and not break down. In the event he came in second, managing to pass Stirling on the third lap which Nanette knew was a real triumph as the Monaco circuit was a difficult one for overtaking. Watching him take the chequered flag, Nanette and the twins cheered loudly before joining the others at lunch.

It was mid-afternoon before a happy Jean-Claude joined them. 'Any food left? I'm starving,' he said.

Nanette, helping Florence in the kitchen, quickly made up a plate of food for him and then followed him into the sitting-room where he was receiving congratulations from everyone.

As Jean-Claude tucked into his late lunch, Mathieu turned to Nanette.

'Are you still planning on spending Grand Prix Sunday up

at the villa? Or now that you and Zac have kissed and made up, are you going to watch from the pit lane?'

'Mathieu, I don't know what Zac has told you, but we certainly haven't kissed and made up – I've still got a lot of questions I'd like him to answer,' Nanette said sharply. 'Does it matter where I am next Sunday then?'

'I've just agreed that Boris can use the apartment next weekend,' Mathieu said. 'Apparently the apartment he was hoping to use isn't available. I've told him Pierre and I will be here and possibly you and Olivia, which isn't a problem for him.'

'Pierre definitely wants to watch the race and Olivia would prefer not to,' Nanette said. 'So, I'll take her up to the villa for the day and leave Pierre with you, if that's OK with you JC?'

'Fine by me,' Jean-Claude assured her. He glanced at Mathieu 'Are you going to Zac's party tomorrow night?'

'Of course, and I'm hoping Nanette is coming as my partner,' Mathieu answered looking at her.

'Thanks, Mathieu, but I've decided not to go,' Nanette said.

Mathieu looked disappointed but merely said, 'That's a shame, but if you change your mind I'll be leaving here about nine thirty. You know Zac's parties never take off until late.'

The night of Zac's party on board his yacht, Monaco Old Port was a mass of twinkling lights from the yachts and the restaurants that lined the harbour. Grand Prix fever was definitely in the air as Monaco slipped into play mode for the biggest week of the year. After the laid back atmosphere of the weekend, it was clear the big boys were now in town ready to party.

Music from several parties already in full swing on various boats floated up on the sultry air. Couples strolled nonchalantly past the luxury yachts, stopping occasionally to gaze inboard in the hope of seeing a famous face or two amongst all the glamorous people.

Standing on the balcony surveying the scene below her, Nanette took in the atmosphere. Whereas it had once been commonplace in her life she was now so detached from the social scene, that watching it held something of a surreal quality for her.

'I'm off. Sure you won't change your mind?' Mathieu asked, appearing unexpectedly at her side.

Nanette shook her head.

'Enjoy yourself. You look very smart, by the way, in your tuxedo.'

'Thanks.' Mathieu hesitated for a second, as though about to say something else, changed his mind and left.

Nanette heard him open the door and was surprised to hear Jean-Claude's voice saying hello.

'What are you doing here, Papa?' Mathieu asked. 'Aren't you coming to Zac's party either?'

'Thought Nanette might like some company tonight,' Jean-Claude said. 'Enjoy the party,' and he closed the door behind Mathieu.

Joining Nanette on the balcony, Jean-Claude smiled at her.

'Great atmosphere down there.'

Nanette nodded. 'Yes. Can I get you a drink or anything?'

'Maybe in a minute, but first I would like to talk to you.'

Jean-Claude glanced at her before continuing quietly, 'I think you should make an appearance at Zac's party tonight. If only for five minutes.'

'Oh, JC,' Nanette sighed.

'Seeing Zac recently was difficult and upset you I know,' Jean-Claude said, 'but going tonight would be another step to getting the past behind you. Zac has expressed a desire to be friends, and his guests are unlikely to create a scene or be rude to you in front of him.'

There was silence as Nanette gazed out unseeingly over the harbour. Knowing that Jean-Claude was right didn't help and she shrugged helplessly as she turned to face him.

'Why don't you go and put on a party dress and we'll go together?' Jean-Claude said gently. 'We don't have to stay long and I promise not to leave your side.'

As Nanette still hesitated, he added, 'It will be fine. Go and change. I'll have a word with Florence to keep an ear out for the twins, but I'm sure they'll be fast asleep by now anyway.'

In her room, Nanette stood uncertainly in front of her wardrobe wondering which dress to wear. She rejected the one she'd worn to accompany Jean-Claude to the Café de Paris as being too dressy and chose instead a sleeveless white one with a lace bolero jacket over the shoulders.

'Do I look OK?' she asked Jean-Claude anxiously as she rejoined him in the sitting-room.

'Nanette, you always look lovely to me whatever you're wearing,' Jean-Claude said quietly.

Struck by the sincere intensity in his voice, Nanette looked at him in surprise before smiling at him shyly and leading the way out of the apartment.

Together they walked past yacht after yacht, each one positively humming with revellers. Everywhere there was noise, laughter, music and glamorous women.

The sudden strident noise of police sirens as several police cars streaked their way along the Boulevard Hercules 1st frightened Nanette and she looked around quickly.

'Probably heading for the auto-route,' Jean-Claude said. 'Hope it's nothing too serious.'

Slipping her shoes off at the end of the gangplank and stepping on to the teak deck of *Pole Position*, Nanette had a sudden attack of nerves and would have run back down to the embankment, if Jean-Claude hadn't unexpectedly taken her hand at that moment, making escape impossible.

The main cabin of the boat was bursting with people and, as they squeezed their way through the throng, Nanette saw several people she knew. She returned a quiet 'hello' to the ones who acknowledged her and did her best not to mind the ones who deliberately turned their backs.

Jean-Claude took two glasses of champagne from the steward at the small bar and handed her one.

Nanette looked around her curiously as she sipped her drink.

'What do you think of the makeover Zac had done earlier this year?' Jean-Claude asked.

'Umm not sure,' Nanette replied evasively. 'Bit too ostentatious for my taste. Wonder where Zac is?'

'Probably out on deck. Shall we go and look?' When Nanette nodded, Jean-Claude took her by the hand again and they made their way through one of the open doors on to the side deck.

Outside they could see Zac and Mathieu up in the bow talking to Boris. By mutual, unspoken consent, Nanette and Jean-Claude stayed where they were. Neither of them wanted to have to make small talk with Boris.

As they stood sipping their drinks and watching the other

party guests, Nanette slowly relaxed. Just as they were about to return to the main cabin, Evie came up to speak to them.

'Hi. I thought it was you. Isn't it a great party? I've been talking to one of the racing drivers, but now he's looking for Zac. He's got a message for him from his technical support team. Apparently the police have stopped the Formula 1 car transporters up on the auto-route for a random search.'

'Nothing unusual in that,' Nanette said. 'It happens quite a lot. Never found anything yet.'

'Oh, but this time they reckon they've had a tip-off and they're searching them all from top to bottom. They seem pretty certain of finding something.' Evie said. 'Look my friend is telling Zac the news now.'

Nanette looked across in time to catch the concerned look Zac exchanged with Boris and Mathieu. Mathieu moved away from the others and began to push his way towards the stern.

Nanette felt a sudden knot of apprehension tighten in her stomach and she moved closer to Jean-Claude. Gently she felt for his hand and held it tightly as they watched Mathieu run down the gangplank before being swallowed up by the crowds still thronging the harbour side, and disappearing from view.

CHAPTER FIVE

Standing on the deck in silence watching Mathieu running away into the night, Nanette felt Jean-Claude's tension as he held her hand.

Nanette glanced around. The party seemed to have come to a premature end with the news of the police raid on the Formula 1 transporters. The deck was still vibrating from the disco music playing in the main cabin but people were leaving, including Boris and his entourage.

'Shall we go?' Nanette asked Jean-Claude quietly.

He nodded in answer and they turned to make their way back to the gangplank.

Nanette, hoping that they would be able to leave unnoticed, was disconcerted to see Zac standing in the stern saying goodnight to people.

'Nanette, Jean-Claude, I'm sorry you're leaving. Can't you both stay longer? I haven't even had a chance to dance with you yet, Nanette. Another glass of champagne perhaps?'

Nanette glanced at him sharply. The last thing she wanted was to dance with Zac.

'*Non*,' Jean-Claude said brusquely. 'I need to find Mathieu.

Perhaps you can tell me where he's gone?' And Jean-Claude glared at Zac.

'How would I know?' Zac said.

'Because I believe you've involved my son in one of your suspect business enterprises,' Jean-Claude said angrily.

Zac looked at him steadily. 'Mathieu is a businessman – he makes his own decisions as to the deals he gets involved in. No-one twists his arm.'

'So, is he is mixed up with you and the Russian in something then?' Jean-Claude demanded.

Zac sighed.

'Jean-Claude, if Mathieu has chosen not to confide in you about his business, I can't help you. Now, are you sure I can't persuade you to stay?' and he looked at Nanette hopefully.

She shook her head and moved away to retrieve her high-heeled sandals from the jumble of footwear in the basket placed at the head of the gangplank.

Slipping them on, she saw Jean-Claude move closer to Zac and place a hand on his shoulder before leaning towards him and saying something that was clearly intended for his ears alone.

Zac's face darkened and he vehemently shrugged Jean-Claude's hand off his shoulder before turning away and making for the bar in the main cabin.

Both Nanette and Jean-Claude were silent as they made their way along the embankment to the apartment, each lost in their own thoughts. Jean-Claude took her arm as they prepared to cross the road.

'Let's have a coffee before I see you home,' he said.

The pavement café at the bottom of Rue Princess Caroline was noisy with late night revellers as Nanette and Jean-

Claude sat at a small table and ordered their *café noisettes*.

'Try not to worry too much about Mathieu,' Nanette said gently. 'Didn't he tell you that things would be clearer to everyone in a couple of months?'

Jean-Claude nodded.

'Well then, try and trust him for a bit longer. Difficult I know.'

As Nanette looked at him sympathetically, he reached out and squeezed her hand. 'I know you're right.' He shook his head as he looked at her. 'I just wish I didn't have this fear in the pit of my stomach.'

Mathieu wasn't home when Nanette took the twins to school the next morning.

Strolling back Nanette wondered where Mathieu was. When her mobile rang she answered it quickly, half expecting it to be him, but it was Jean-Claude.

'Have you seen Mathieu?'

'No. And according to Florence his bed hadn't been slept in,' Nanette said. 'Have you heard anything more about the raid?'

'Apparently the police did find something, but nobody knows what exactly – although rumour has it as a case full of money.'

'Did they arrest anyone?'

'A couple of the truck drivers have been spoken to but the motor-homes and transporters were all allowed to park up without any problems. The Formula 1 circus keeps to a very tight schedule as you know, and nothing must interfere with race week. The police are still up on site searching some of them.'

There was a short pause before Jean-Claude continued, 'Will you let me know when Mathieu returns?'

'Yes, of course.'

Replacing the phone in her bag, Nanette wandered slowly along a side street filled with various stalls selling Formula 1 racing paraphernalia and fast food.

Even at this early hour there were fans strolling around, mixing with the locals trying to go about their normal lives despite the inconvenience of barriers and streets filled with seating stands. Tomorrow, a practice day, the road around town and along the harbour would be closed to traffic as the drivers began to get to grips with driving around the narrow winding street circuit at over a hundred miles an hour.

Although it was several years since Nanette had been in Monaco for the Grand Prix, it was still all so familiar. Walking past the souvenir stands and the touts already up and about trying to sell tickets for lunch on practice day at restaurants with views of the circuit, she even recognized one or two people and smiled briefly in their direction.

Ferrari red was the dominant colour of the bunting hanging from balconies and the smell of crêpes cooking on a mobile catering stall on the corner competing with the usual breakfast smell of fresh croissants from the *boulangerie*, was hard to resist.

Nanette pushed open the glass door of the foyer to the apartment building and pressed the lift button. The two concierges behind the reception desk stopped in mid conversation as she entered, but not before Nanette heard the words 'Monsieur Mathieu'.

As she walked into the sitting-room, Florence appeared and pointed to Mathieu's bedroom. 'Mathieu has returned.

He is sleeping and asked not to be disturbed,' she said quietly.

Quickly, Nanette rang Jean-Claude to tell him the news.

'I'll be there in five minutes,' he said.

It was lunchtime before Mathieu appeared in the sitting-room and both Jean-Claude and Nanette stared at him.

Jean-Claude immediately started to fire questions at him about the raid.

'So, they found a suitcase of money? It's not a crime to keep your money in cash,' Mathieu said, going to the fridge and pouring a glass of milk.

'Depends on where the money came from – and where it's going,' Jean-Claude replied.

'One of the mechanics apparently had a lucky bet on the Spanish Grand Prix. He simply hadn't had time to bank his winnings.'

'OK,' Jean-Claude said. 'We'll accept that story. Now, tell us why you ran from Zac's party when you heard about the police raid.'

His face was impassive as he watched Mathieu, waiting for his reply.

'Coincidence. I was about to leave anyway. I'd arranged to meet someone at the Automobile Club and I was late.'

Mathieu simply shrugged as Jean-Claude stared disbelievingly at him. 'Interrogation finished? I need a shower and then I promised Pierre I'd meet him from school, take him down to the pits and Zac would introduce him to a couple of the drivers.'

'*Non*. It is not finished,' Jean-Claude shouted at his son. 'Not until you tell me the truth about what is going on.'

Mathieu shook his head as he looked at his father. 'I can't tell you anything. But if it's the family reputation you're worried about, don't.'

'It's you, I'm worried about, not the family name,' Jean-Claude said angrily. 'Scandals can be lived through, but the repercussions are never nice.'

'Oh believe me,' Mathieu said grimly, 'the repercussions in this case will hit a lot of people in Monaco.' And with that cryptic remark, he disappeared back into his room to get ready to go out.

Jean-Claude looked at Nanette, worry lines etched on his face.

'At least he's finally admitted to being involved in something,' he sighed. 'Did you believe him – about the money and the Automobile Club?'

'He could have had an appointment I suppose but. . . .' Nanette shook her head. 'I don't know.'

'I've got an appointment of my own tomorrow,' Jean-Claude said quietly, glancing at Mathieu's closed bedroom door. 'I'm meeting a private detective to have Mathieu followed for a couple of weeks. I need to know what is going on.'

'Oh JC – be careful. If Mathieu discovers what you are up to he'll be furious.'

'I'll have to risk it. I'm not convinced he's not in real trouble. I just want some reassurance that he's not getting out of his depth with the wrong crowd. I also want to be prepared in case of. . . .' Jean-Claude left the sentence unfinished, as he shrugged his shoulders and shook his head in despair.

Life in the jungle settled into a pattern for Vanessa as she and Ralph became absorbed into the routine of village life. Ralph, busy helping and recording the building of a small dam on a river near the village, disappeared early every morning with the men, leaving Vanessa to spend her days with Angela and the other women.

Evenings were spent in the large communal hut where, as honoured guests, they were fêted with the best the villagers could provide and entertained with traditional songs and music.

In their hammocks at night in the small hut allocated to them, Ralph told Vanessa about his worries for the village.

'They seem to think this dam we're building to help with the gold panning is going to be their path to untold riches. And now some sleaze from Rio has appeared on the scene telling them his boss will help to fund enlarging the mine and sell the gold on for them – all for a big fat rake off, of course.' He shook his head. 'They know the mercury he's going to provide for separating the gold is poisonous and so bad for the forest, but they hear of other villages prospering and they want to do the same. The fact that they'll probably end up polluting their water supply, poisoning the fish and eroding the forest even more doesn't seem to be an issue with them.'

'Can't you persuade them to stick to just panning for gold without the mercury?' Vanessa asked.

'I've tried. But they're desperate and see this as the only way to survive. I wish I could think of some other way they could make the money to buy the essentials like stock and seeds so they can carry on farming in the traditional way.'

'Eco-tourism like the village we stayed in?' Vanessa asked.

'The villagers aren't keen on the idea of lots of strangers. Besides they're so poor they don't have the money to even improve their own basic living conditions. And being so deep in the jungle here, it wouldn't be easy to organize. I know, I had a few problems getting us here. Most of those eco-camps are within two or three hours of the Amazon.'

He sighed. 'The trouble is we're here for such a short time there's not a lot we can do. The dam should be finished tomorrow, maybe I'll get a chance to talk to the head shaman.'

He leant across and gave Vanessa a kiss.

'Nearly forget to tell you: Luigi, the guide, has offered to take us to see the young dolphins. It's a three-hour trek to get to where they're being born but should be well worth it.' And Ralph smiled happily at his wife.

The next morning Ralph left as usual and Vanessa joined Angela and the other women for the daily chores. Today, in addition to the normal cooking and husbandry of the small animals that roamed around the village, they were planning to plant seedlings.

As ever, the humidity in the jungle was high and Vanessa struggled to keep pace with Angela and the others as they went to collect the seedlings from the large government controlled farm where they'd been grown.

It proved to be a long hard day as they planted the small trees on cleared forestland previously grazed by cattle.

From time to time thunderstorms rolled across the sky and torrential rain forced them to stop work and seek shelter. During one of these breaks Vanessa noticed that a couple of the women were muttering unhappily together.

'They have nothing,' Angela explained. 'Life is getting harder and all they hear is how we must take care of the forest. Who is going to take care of us? We have to survive too.' She shook her head. 'We have a school now but what work is there going to be for the children?'

'Will a bigger gold mine help?' Vanessa asked. 'Ralph says

it's not the answer, but what do you think?'

Angela bit her bottom lip before replying, 'If it was a legal gold mine it would help more. But the wrong people will benefit from it.'

Vanessa gazed at her horrified. Did Ralph know he was building a dam to help an illegal gold mine operate?

Before she could ask any more the rain stopped and the women began to move back out on to the wetland.

'If we are to survive living off the land we need more help,' Angela added quietly, as she handed Vanessa a trowel and another box of seedlings.

Thoughtfully Vanessa began the rhythmic business of planting the tiny trees – dig hole, drop seedling in, cover and press, on to the next – while trying to work out how Ralph would respond to the news about the mine.

It was late afternoon when Vanessa removed her hat and pushed her damp hair back from her face. Her clothes were wet and sticking to her body and she remembered longingly the delights of a cool shower. At least it would soon be time to return to the village and help prepare the evening meal in the shade of the trees surrounding the encampment.

As the women were gathering their things together, one of the young native boys returning from the day's work on the dam, ran up to Angela and said something to her urgently. Vanessa felt a tremor of fear pass through her body as Angela glanced across at her, a look of concern on her face, before walking towards her.

'What's happened? Has Ralph had an accident?' Fear made her voice sound shrill even to her own ears.

'Ralph has been taken ill,' Angela said quietly. 'The men are bringing him back to the village.'

'I must go to him,' Vanessa said, panic-stricken, and went to run towards the huddle of men approaching the village.

Angela placed a restraining hand on her.

'Wait here,' she said gently. 'Let the men deal with it.'

Vanessa's heart was in her mouth as she watched the group approaching. She forced herself to stay still as two of the village men carried an unconscious Ralph on a makeshift stretcher into the compound before carefully placing him in the medicine man's hut.

Early Sunday morning and the balcony doors of Mathieu's apartment were wide open. Nanette stood for a few moments watching the thousands of people making their way to highly prized seats in the harbour side grandstands.

Yacht crews on the luxury boats moored so close to each other their fenders barely able to keep the gleaming hulls apart, were busy serving strong coffee and croissants to guests who had partied the night away on board.

Nanette, glancing towards *Pole Position* knew that Zac would have been up at the crack of dawn to prepare for the day and wasn't surprised to see just the crew moving around the boat's fore deck. It had always been one of Zac's unwritten rules – no guests on board the Saturday night before the Grand Prix.

Looking out across the starting grid, she could see cameramen and journalists milling around eager to get an exclusive early interview with anyone willing to express an opinion on the way they thought the day's race would go.

She'd been away for so long she'd almost forgotten the excitement Monaco generated on race weekend, both on the track and off, as the jet set indulged themselves with a combination of high octane living and fast cars.

The sound of highly tuned engines being revved was beginning to fill the air – a sign of the frenzied activity that Nanette knew would already be taking place out of sight in the garages at the back of the pit lane.

She turned as she heard the apartment door open and close. Mathieu.

'That's Olivia sorted for the day,' he said, joining Nanette on the balcony. 'A day at the Aqua Splash Park with friends is much more to her liking than watching a boring car race.'

He leant on the balcony and surveyed the crowds and the activity down below him.

'Make you nostalgic for your old life?' he asked, glancing at her. 'All those VIP parties and events you and Zac used to go to.'

'No, not really,' Nanette answered. 'It seems a lifetime away, so much has happened. It was fun at the time but things change – I've changed.'

'Things certainly do change,' Mathieu said, so quietly that Nanette barely heard him. He was silent for a few moments simply staring down into the pits area.

'Mathieu, is everything all right?' Nanette eventually asked, gently. 'Is there anything I can help with?'

'Thanks, Nanette,' Mathieu said. 'Things are a bit difficult at the moment but everything is under control.' He smiled at her before changing the subject, effectively stopping her from asking any questions.

'Should be a good race today. Zac did well qualifying for pole yesterday – let's hope he can stay out in front for the race. Monaco is one circuit he hasn't won.'

'A win today would put him well in the lead for the

championship too,' Nanette said. 'And we all know he's desperate to be world champion,' she added drily. She hesitated before continuing. 'Mathieu, I have to ask, are you sure it's OK with Boris that I stay today?'

Mathieu looked at her surprised. 'Why on earth wouldn't it be?'

Nanette shrugged. 'It's just that I thought Boris wanted the place for him and his cronies. And the plan originally was for me to go to Jean-Claude's, if you remember.'

'It's fine for both you and Pierre to be here. Jean-Claude is coming down too,' Mathieu said. 'So relax and enjoy the day.'

The apartment bell rang at that moment and Mathieu turned to greet the first of his guests. Boris acknowledged Nanette with a *'Bonjour madam'* and a tilt of his head before roughly ruffling Pierre's hair – an action that had the boy dodging out of his way. Within minutes, the rest of Boris's party had arrived and Nanette and Pierre were ignored for the next hour.

To Nanette's relief Jean-Claude arrived just as lunch was being served and together they sat at one of the small round tables Florence had set up on the balcony. Pierre, more interested in watching the scenes below than eating his lunch, had the binoculars trained on the pit lane.

The atmosphere on the balcony appeared to be one of general conviviality. Florence was handing food around and Mathieu was busy organizing drinks for everyone.

'Mathieu seems in good spirits today,' Jean-Claude said, glancing across at him.

'Yes,' Nanette said. 'Although something is definitely worrying him.'

Jean-Claude raised his eyebrows questioningly.

'I don't know what, JC, but he did tell me everything was under control earlier this morning,' Nanette said quietly with an anxious glance at Pierre.

'Any news from Vanessa and Ralph?' Jean-Claude asked, taking the hint and deftly changing the subject.

'We had a letter from Mum yesterday,' Pierre said, without removing his gaze from the cars lining up on the grid. 'She'd given it to someone in the jungle to post when they went to a big town. Wish we could e-mail her but the village they are in doesn't have electricity.'

'Did she say how things were going?' Jean-Claude asked.

'Just that she was seeing some amazing things and as soon as she could she'd write again.'

The cars took off for their formation lap at that moment and Pierre pulled the official ear-protectors Zac had given him over his ears. By the time the warm-up lap was completed and the cars were back on the grid ready for the off, Boris and his guests were crowded on the balcony waiting for the start.

Everyone gazed as one by one the red starting lights went out and then the earth-shattering sound of high-performance cars making for the Saint Dévote bend at high speed before disappearing up the hill towards the Casino, blasted through the apartment. A loud cheer went up as Zac, making a perfect start, kept his lead, and within seconds had disappeared from view, leaving the cars behind him to juggle for better positions as best they could.

Now everyone's attention switched to one of the large TV screens set up by the harbour. As she watched Zac fly past the Café de Paris on his way towards the Horseshoe Bend for the first time, Nanette hoped that the race would be trouble free. Monaco Grand Prix might be a firm favourite with the drivers because of the challenges the street circuit gave them, but Nanette knew that simple fact made it more dangerous than any other racetrack.

Racing out of the tunnel and coming back down towards the harbour Zac was continuing to pull away from the cars behind him and had already put fifteen seconds between himself and the last car when he roared past the apartment again starting his second lap.

Boris and two of his guests moved back into the sitting-room soon after the start and began talking quietly amongst themselves, occasionally glancing at the race on the small television on the sideboard. Nanette, fetching a bottle of water from the kitchen, strained to hear what they were saying as she walked past but caught only the words 'money' and 'yacht'.

Zac stayed comfortably ahead for the race, his team providing him with two perfect pit stops to keep him in the lead. Nanette, watching him climb the hill past the Hérmitage Hotel on his sixty-ninth lap knew that with just nine laps left, he was finally on target to win the Monaco Grand Prix with a nineteen second lead over the car in second place.

But then on lap seventy-two disaster struck. The driver in fourth position misjudged La Rascasse corner and drove into the wall. The uninjured, but frustrated driver, climbed out of his car, shaking his head sadly at the crowds. Yellow flags were waved and the safety car was soon out on the track and the drivers were forced to slow down. Under racing rules all cars had to keep to their current position – overtaking was not allowed whilst the safety car was out in front.

By the time the track was cleared of the crashed car and its debris, there were only two laps of the race left and all the remaining cars had bunched up behind each other. As the safety car left the track everyone watching held their breath willing Zac to stay out of danger – and out front.

As he negotiated the chicane before the old swimming pool complex for the final time, the second and third cars were just seconds behind him but it was Zac who rounded La Rascasse and roared across the finishing line first to take the chequered flag.

Nanette joined in the spontaneous cheering that erupted along the balcony. Despite all that had happened between them she couldn't help but be pleased for him.

'Can I go down and watch the presentation?' Pierre asked, excitedly.

'We'll come with you,' Jean-Claude answered knowing Nanette wouldn't let Pierre go alone.

Downstairs, the mechanics and other team members were crowding around and Prince Albert and the rest of his family had appeared, ready to present the trophies.

Nanette, Jean-Claude and Pierre managed to squeeze into a small space alongside the presentation stand. Standing there watching the ceremony as a jubilant Zac received his trophy from Prince Albert and held it aloft, Nanette felt a certain sense of *déjà vu* washing over her.

How many times had she watched similar ceremonies and then been at Zac's side as he'd partied through the night? Now, as the champagne was shaken and sprayed everywhere, she joined in with the general noise of the victory celebrations, but her feelings were somehow detached from what was going on around her.

Running across to give the champagne bottle to his mechanics, Zac waved to Pierre and saw Nanette standing alongside him.

Immediately he changed course and came over to them.

'Congratulations, Zac,' Jean-Claude said.

'Thanks.'

Zac turned to Nanette. 'Dinner tomorrow night. Eight o'clock. No excuses. I need to talk to you urgently.'

And he was gone back to his mechanics, leaving Nanette speechless – and angry with his assumption that of course she would obey his order.

A loud bang outside the apartment block woke Nanette with a jolt early Monday morning. Startled, it took her a second or two to realize it was the workmen starting the long process of dismantling barriers and stands and returning Monaco to its normal state for the next ten months.

Lying in bed for a few moments Nanette thought about Zac and his dinner 'invitation'. She had talked about it to Jean-Claude last night before he returned to his villa.

'I still have questions I'd like Zac to answer,' she'd said. 'Maybe he's decided to talk to me.'

'Perhaps he just wants to take you out to dinner and knew you wouldn't willingly consider it,' Jean-Claude said. 'But in my experience Zac Ewart never does anything without a reason,' he added quietly.

All day, as she went about her normal routine Nanette found herself thinking about Jean-Claude's remark. By 8.00 p.m. though, when Zac rang the apartment bell, she'd convinced herself that their shared past was the reason Zac wanted to take her out for dinner.

'Where are we going?' Nanette asked, as the lift took them down to the ground floor.

'We're eating on board *Pole Position*,' Zac said. 'I've got a terrific chef this year and he's promised me a meal to remember.'

Once on board, the yacht's crew sprang into action, ensuring everything went smoothly. Sipping her champagne and nibbling canapés, Nanette looked around the main saloon as Zac pressed a couple of hidden buttons on the wall. Simultaneously the side windows opened letting in a gentle sea breeze and romantic piano music filtered through the sound system.

Zac, still on a high from his win, seemed determined to wine and dine himself back into Nanette's favour.

When Nanette tried to ask him something about the accident, he placed a gentle finger against her lips.

'Not this evening, Nanette. Tonight is a new beginning.' He clicked his champagne glass against hers. '*Santé*'

Nanette looked at him, exasperated. 'But I still have questions I want answered and you said you wanted to talk to me urgently.'

'I do. Later. Now come and eat. We've got lobster especially for you.'

As he helped her to a generous portion of her favourite dish, Nanette's thoughts drifted back three years, to a time when evenings like this with Zac had been the norm.

Candles in elaborate candelabra casting shadows, seductive music playing in the background, the moon shining on the Mediterranean. A perfect setting for romance. Nanette glanced at Zac. What exactly was he playing at tonight?

'Are you doing anything special for your birthday this year?' Zac asked.

Nanette shook her head. 'No, nothing planned.' She didn't

add she hadn't celebrated her birthday properly in the years since the accident. The two anniversaries were too close together.

'I remember we always used to celebrate it early as I was racing. I'm going to Canada straight after the UK Grand Prix this weekend so I'll miss it again. You'll have to think of this as an early birthday treat,' Zac said.

'So long as you don't plan on presenting me with a car later,' Nanette said shortly. 'Because—' She stopped in mid-sentence and stared at him.

'Because what?' Zac asked, glancing at her curiously.

'Because I'd have to decline of course,' Nanette said. Carefully she placed her napkin on the table and stood up.

'Zac, I've had a lovely meal, but I think I'd like to leave now if you don't mind.'

Surprised, Zac followed her as she went to leave the saloon, and caught her by the hand.

'At least dance with me for old times' sake,' he said.

And before she realized what was happening, Nanette was in his arms and the two of them were on deck swaying to 'Lady in Red' a favourite of theirs from the past.

As Zac held her close it was as if the last three years apart had never happened. He appeared to have conveniently forgotten the trauma, the hurt and the broken heart he'd left her with. But Nanette hadn't and even if old emotions that she'd thought were dead forever were rising to the surface, she wasn't about to give in to them.

When Zac began placing gentle kisses on her head a tremor of anger flooded through her body.

'Zac, stop it now.' Nanette pushed him away. 'I'm leaving – don't try and stop me again!'

Zac shrugged. 'I just thought maybe you'd like to forget the past – put it behind us.'

Ignoring him, Nanette began to make her way to the gangway. More shaken than she cared to admit, the only thing she wanted to do was get off the yacht.

She'd thought she was over Zac and yet here he was, proving he still had the power to stir her.

She was on the gangplank when he called her name. Swallowing hard she turned her head to look at him, her hand gripping the gangway rope tightly for support as Zac spoke.

'I invited you here tonight for a reason. You see, Nanette, I have a proposal for you. One to which I hope very much you will say yes.'

CHAPTER SIX

'How did your dinner date with Zac go?' Mathieu asked. 'Are you two finally friends again?'

Mathieu asked his questions as he, Nanette and the twins walked around the headland towards the open-air cinema. The twins, excited at the prospect of seeing the latest *Pirates of the Caribbean* film had rushed ahead.

'Not really,' Nanette replied slowly. 'Nothing's really changed. Zac certainly hasn't.'

She was still in turmoil from the evening she'd spent with Zac. As for his proposal, she hadn't yet discussed it with anybody.

She glanced sideways at Mathieu, unsure if he was the right person to confide in about what had happened on board *Pole Position* between her and Zac, but she needed to talk to someone and because the twins were involved, Mathieu did have a right to know what Zac had proposed last night.

'Come back and have another glass of champagne,' Zac had urged. 'I really need to talk to you.'

Standing on the gangplank Nanette had been determined.

'No thanks, Zac. I don't want any more to drink. Whatever you've got to say to me can be said out here.'

Holding her breath Nanette waited for him to speak. She was determined not to let Zac see how shaken she was. And how unbelievably angry she was with him over his actions – both past and present.

'Come back and work for me, Nanette.'

His unexpected request fell into a lengthening silence as Nanette gazed at him. All this wining and dining and faux romancing was because he wanted her to work for him? Not because he wanted them to be a couple again as she'd foolishly begun to imagine.

'What?' She looked at him in disbelief.

'I'm starting a holiday business and I need someone I can trust totally,' Zac said.

'I've got a job – looking after the twins. And when Vanessa and Ralph return from their Amazon adventure, I shall go back to the UK with them.'

'Come on, Nanette – you're capable of much more than playing nursemaid to a couple of kids. You were the best PA I ever had.'

'If I was that good, why no word, no job offer from you before – when I needed all the help I could get?' Nanette asked angrily.

'I cut back on my business activities when I realized you weren't going to be around for a long time,' Zac said, shrugging. 'I was too busy racing and simply didn't have the time to find a new PA.'

'And now you've got time for a new venture?'

'This time I'm trying to invest in a business that I can work at when I give up racing.'

'You're giving up racing?' Nanette asked shocked.

'Not immediately, but I don't fancy being the oldest driver on the circuit fighting for a drive. Realistically, I suppose, I've got another two or three years, but if I don't win the championship this season' – Zac grimaced – 'who knows? I might just walk away from it all in October.'

He paused and smiled at her. 'I also thought it would be an ideal opportunity to try and make up for the hurt that I've caused you in the past. We could both go places with this new business.'

Zac looked at her expectantly, waiting for her response.

Nanette sighed. Zac could sound so plausible when he turned on the charm. She'd seen it work in the past when he'd wanted his own way over something. But not this time, not with her.

'Apart from the fact that I'm not looking for another job – I'm happy caring for the twins – working for you again is not something I'd ever thought about.'

'Will you think about it now?' Zac persisted. 'The twins are growing up they won't need you forever.'

'You don't need me either, Zac.'

'Oh but, Nanette, I do,' Zac said, once again reaching out to take hold of her hands and squeeze them tightly. 'I leave for Silverstone tomorrow and then I'm back here for three days before I fly out to Canada. Please think about it while I'm away. We'll have supper next week and you can give me your decision then.'

'I don't need time to think Zac. I don't—'

'Shh.' Zac effectively stopped her by placing his fingers firmly against her lips. 'Next week.'

'Goodnight, Zac.' Once again, she turned away from him,

stepping back on to the gangplank to leave. Zac didn't try to stop her this time.

'I'll see you home,' he said. 'Just give me two minutes while I fetch something from my cabin.'

Feeling the need to put some firm ground underneath her feet, Nanette jumped off the yacht's gangplank and stood waiting on the quay.

Standing there, watching the evening activity of the harbour, Nanette felt curiously light-headed. The events of the past hour had been totally unexpected, but she was pleased she'd kept her cool and been able to be so resolute in facing up to Zac despite her hammering heart.

'Here you are – some bedtime reading,' Zac said, reappearing with a large envelope marked *Vacances au Soleil* and bulging with papers. 'At least have a look at it while I'm away,' he said, when Nanette tried to refuse to take it. 'It might help change your mind.'

Nanette had thrown the envelope on to the table in her room intending to ignore it and simply hand it back to Zac next week, but curiosity had got the better of her and the next morning she'd opened it.

Now, as she and Mathieu caught up with the twins near the cinema, she began to tell him about the contents of the envelope.

'*Vacances au Soleil* is apparently going to be an exclusive holiday club, which will, for a large amount of money naturally, arrange dream holidays for their members, anywhere in the world. Dubai, St Tropez, Rio, Sun City and of course Monaco.'

'And Zac wants you to run the operation for him?'

Nanette nodded. 'Yes. Initially the office would be on board *Pole Position*. And, according to the job description he'd thoughtfully put in the envelope, he wants me to travel to inspect the places and make sure they're exclusive enough. Starting next month.'

'Could be fun,' Mathieu said.

'He's conveniently brushed aside the events of the last three years – and the fact that I look after the twins,' Nanette said, crossly. 'It's only a few weeks before the long summer break begins. Even if I was tempted, which I'm not, there is no way I could possibly let Vanessa and Ralph – or you – down in that way.'

Mathieu was silent for a moment.

'Do you have any plans for the future? The twins are growing up – they won't need a nanny for much longer. Maybe Zac would keep the job open for you? Or you could start with just an hour or so a day while the twins are at school.'

Nanette gazed at him exasperated.

'Mathieu, I don't want to work for Zac again. I don't belong in his world any more. And I don't think I even like him any more. I certainly don't trust him.'

Mathieu paid for their tickets and sent the twins off to buy a snack from the refreshment cabin before turning to answer her.

'I can't tell you the details but this "thing" I'm involved with is getting more complicated,' he said quietly. 'I could do with some inside help.' He glanced at her. 'You working for Zac, having access to papers and his associates, might be very useful to me.'

'Are you saying Zac is involved in this "thing"?' Nanette demanded.

Mathieu didn't answer directly, simply giving a slight shrug of his shoulders.

'Is Jean-Claude right then, in thinking you've become embroiled in something illicit?' Nanette asked worriedly.

Mathieu sighed. 'It's not as simple as being illicit or illegal. And now to complicate matters even more, I think I'm being followed.'

The twins arrived back at that moment clutching crisps and popcorn and clamouring to go and find their seats.

'Come on, Dad, the film starts in five minutes,' Pierre said.

Mathieu gave Nanette an apologetic glance. 'We'll talk later – let's go watch pirates!'

Sifting under a cloudless sky as dusk fell over the Mediterranean, Nanette tried to concentrate on the film but not even the swashbuckling Johnny Depp could take her mind off the problems of the man sitting next to her, his arm casually around her shoulders.

And as for his, 'I think I'm being followed' statement – how could she possibly tell him the person behind that particular problem was his own father?

The night she spent sitting in the shaman's hut beside a delirious Ralph was one of the longest of Vanessa's life.

For two hours after the native bearers had placed him in the hut, Vanessa had paced up and down outside. Refused admittance by the chief shaman she could do nothing but pray for her husband and wonder what was going on in there.

Nick and Harry, the cameramen, gave her a brief account of what had happened out by the mine.

'Ralph didn't feel well all morning, said his stomach was

hurting. He ate very little lunch before he was sick.'

'Why on earth didn't he return to camp?' Vanessa said.

'Thought he'd be better working through it,' Harry answered.

'Said he must have eaten a grub or some other local delicacy last night that didn't agree with him. Once he'd been sick he did seem a bit brighter. We did manage to persuade him to have a short snooze before work started again and he seemed better for it.'

Vanessa listened horrified as Nick then told her about the boulder that had slipped as the men had tried to manoeuvre it into position for the dam. Breaking the wooden stakes they were using to guide it into position it had fallen, giving Ralph's head a glancing blow and knocking him unconscious into the stream.

Listening to Nick's matter-of-fact account of what had happened, Vanessa remembered the words of the tourist in the eco-camp. 'All the money in the world won't get you out of the jungle in a hurry'.

What if Ralph didn't respond to whatever mumbo jumbo they were saying and administering to him in there? How was she going to get him to a proper hospital?

As if reading her thoughts, Harry said, 'If he hasn't regained consciousness by tomorrow, we'll get him carried down to the tributary and hire a canoe to take him to the Amazon River itself. Then hopefully we can get him to a hospital in one of the large towns.'

Vanessa looked at him in despair.

'But that will take days.'

There was a second or two's pause, before Nick said, 'Let's pray it won't be necessary. I'm told some of these natural

105

medicines the natives use are amazingly effective.'

Both Nick and Harry stayed with her until Angela appeared with some food for Vanessa and insisted she ate it.

'It is going to be a long night,' she said quietly. 'You will need all your strength.'

Angela was still with her when the head shaman came out and said Vanessa could finally see Ralph. Fearful of how Ralph would look, Vanessa clutched Angela's hand and walked slowly into the hut.

'You stay with him tonight?' the shaman asked. 'I show you what to do.'

Looking at Ralph's injured face and his battered body, daubed with what Vanessa took to be some sort of native ointment and protected in places with primitive dressings, she forced herself to concentrate on what she had to do for Ralph.

'The next few hours are critical,' Angela said.

The medicine man and Angela showed her how to gently bathe Ralph's cuts and bruises with a sticky substance that Angela explained was a sap taken from trees in the forest.

'Sangre de Grado – it is good,' Angela assured Vanessa. 'You see tomorrow, Ralph will look better. He will be better.'

Vanessa did a lot of praying that night as she tended to Ralph. Applying cooling compresses to a large bump on his temple and gently stroking his hand, she willed him to regain consciousness.

Around two o'clock he began to mumble and restlessly moved his head from side to side. Quickly Vanessa changed the compress for a cooler, fresh one. As she gently held it in place she scrutinized his face for any further glimmer of life but he'd lapsed back into unconsciousness and the long night continued.

At regular intervals one of the native men would appear in the doorway of the hut, stand there looking at Ralph for several seconds, before vanishing back into the darkness. The first time it happened it spooked Vanessa, but as the hours went on she welcomed the fleeting visits.

Dawn was beginning to filter through the canopy of trees surrounding the hut when Ralph finally opened his eyes and smiled at her. Vanessa felt a huge wave of relief sweep through her body and she gave him a gentle kiss.

'Hi, welcome back.'

'Sorry about the dolphins.'

For a moment Vanessa thought Ralph was still delirious before remembering today was the day they were to have trekked to the breeding grounds to see the young dolphins.

She shook her head. 'It doesn't matter. You're more important. How do you feel?'

'Groggy – and thirsty.'

Carefully Vanessa held a cup of water to his lips as Ralph took several sips.

'Do you remember what happened to you?'

'Yes. I was in the way of the boulder when it broke the wooden runners and fell. We were so close to finishing the dam too. Still hopefully today the boys will be able to sort it.'

'Just so long as you're not thinking of joining them,' Vanessa said.

Ralph shook his head and then groaned with the pain it generated.

Vanessa waited a couple of seconds before saying quietly, 'I'm not sure you're well enough to hear this but you need to know.'

Ralph glanced at her puzzled as she took a breath before

continuing, 'Angela was here earlier, talking to me. She doesn't think any of this was an accident.'

Ralph sighed and reached out for her hand.

'I know. Neither do I. The head shaman warned me to be careful a couple of days ago.'

'But why didn't you tell me? The villagers seemed happy to have us around when we arrived,' Vanessa said. 'What's changed?'

'Since the guy from Rio has become involved some of the men have become wary of me filming the village activities. Particularly the dam,' Ralph explained quietly.

'Is that because of the mercury they're going to be using? Will the profits from the gold still go to the village?' Vanessa asked.

Ralph's fingers squeezed hers before saying slowly, 'Not as much as the villagers hope.'

Vanessa was silent, remembering how worried Angela was about the future of the village and its people, how they desperately needed to find a reliable way of sustaining their way of life.

'There must be another way,' Vanessa said thoughtfully. 'Something legal they can do to survive.'

'If we could think of another option, I'd be only too happy to help them set it up,' Ralph said quietly, 'but as far as I can see there is nothing we can do. There's something else. They want us to leave.'

'Are we going to?'

'Not immediately no. I've still got a couple of things I'd like to film. But I've promised to stay away from the dam – which suits me. The less I know about it the better.'

Vanessa stroked his forehead gently.

'How much longer do you think we'll be here?' she asked quietly.

'A week, maybe a bit less – depends on how quickly I get better from this little incident,' Ralph said. 'Could I have another drink please?'

As she held the water to Ralph's lips, Vanessa thought about Ralph's 'little incident'. It was typical of him to play down the seriousness of the accident but Vanessa knew it could have turned out so differently. She could have been a widow before they'd been married even six months.

She smothered a sigh. Another week and then the trek back out of the jungle, back to civilization and proper doctors.

Ralph was regarding her anxiously.

'If you want to leave and wait for me in the eco-camp I'm sure Angela could arrange for a guide.'

'I'm not leaving you,' Vanessa said fiercely. 'We came together and we'll leave together. OK?'

Ralph nodded weakly and closed his eyes. 'Love you,' he whispered as he drifted exhausted back into sleep.

Vanessa sat at his side, still holding his hand, and wishing they were already in the comparative safety of the eco-camp.

Nanette took a deep breath, gripped the steering wheel tightly, and gently pressed the accelerator pedal. As the car began to move forward she found herself hardly daring to breathe.

'Relax,' Jean-Claude said. 'Nothing is going to happen.'

It was Sunday mid-morning and the two of them were on their way to Antibes for lunch, when Jean-Claude had taken an unexpected detour before stopping the car and insisting it was time for Nanette to start driving again.

Getting into the driver's seat was hard but once her seat belt was fastened, Jean-Claude turned the ignition key and waited patiently as Nanette steadied her nerves.

'Drive to the end of the road and I'll take over again, if you want me to,' he said. 'Just take it slowly.'

By the time she'd steered the car the couple of hundred yards to the end of the road without any mishaps, Nanette had managed to take a couple of deep breaths. As she stopped at the T-junction and pulled the handbrake on she glanced across at Jean-Claude.

'Can I go a bit further?' she asked. 'It actually feels good to be behind the wheel again.'

'Of course. If you turn left here and then take the next right we'll be back on the Bord de Mer.'

Nanette eased the car into the stream of traffic and carefully changed gear. By the time she turned on to the Bord de Mer her confidence was returning.

But then a noisy scooter, swerving in and out of the traffic, unnerved her and when the driver clipped her passenger-door wing mirror as he passed too close on the wrong side of the road, she abruptly parked in the first parking space she saw.

She was shaking as she pulled on the handbrake and turned off the ignition before turning to Jean-Claude.

'That wasn't your fault,' he said. 'You must remember how irresponsible the scooter drivers down here are – they cut everyone up from all angles.'

'I'd forgotten,' Nanette said, undoing her seat belt and opening her door. 'But I've had enough. You drive the rest of the way please.'

Twenty minutes later the car was parked and they were

strolling along the ancient ramparts in Antibes on their way to one of Jean-Claude's favourite restaurants. As they settled themselves at a window table Nanette relaxed, she'd been looking forward to spending the day with Jean-Claude from the moment Mathieu had said he was taking the twins out for the day.

'I'll be away for most of next week,' he'd said. 'So I thought I'd treat them to a day's sailing in Italy.'

Jean-Claude, who was in the apartment at the time, had immediately insisted Nanette spend the day with him, an invitation she was happy to accept. It would be an ideal opportunity to talk to JC – to ask his advice.

The restaurant, popular with both locals and tourists, was busy but the staff were attentive and within minutes Nanette and Jean-Claude had aperitifs and the bread basket in front of them and the waiter had disappeared to fetch the bottle of wine Jean-Claude had chosen to accompany their main courses.

'Has the private detective discovered anything?' Nanette asked as she broke off a piece of bread.

'*Non*. Nothing new anyway. Mathieu has had dinner several times at the Automobile Club. Boris was there on one occasion. Zac on another. But my detective wasn't the only one surveying things. He recognized an ex-gendarmerie colleague who now runs an agency in Nice.'

'Was he watching Mathieu as well?'

'Apparently not. He followed Boris when he left. Which makes me wonder, who was paying him to do that?'

'Your man can't ask his ex-colleague?'

'He can ask but he can't tell me. Client confidentiality and all that,' Jean-Claude said, shaking his head.

'Mathieu knows he's being followed, you know,' Nanette said. 'He doesn't know who's arranged it, though,' she added quickly.

Jean-Claude was silent for a few seconds, thoughtfully fingering the stem of his wine glass.

'What a mess,' he sighed. 'If only he'd tell me what was going on I could help. I'm not without connections. I know people in the right places as they say.' He shrugged and looked at Nanette helplessly.

'Mathieu thinks I could help,' she said slowly.

Jean-Claude was instantly alert.

'How? Has he asked you to do something?'

'Zac has – and Mathieu thinks it would be a good idea for me to do it. I think I've already decided what I'm going to do, but I wanted to talk to you about it first.'

Quickly she explained about *Vacances au Soleil* and the job offer that Zac had made her.

As she finished speaking, Jean-Claude reached out for her hand and held it tightly.

'Nanette, listen to me. I can't forbid you to work for Zac, but please don't. I don't care what Mathieu says about it helping him – he is so wrong to try and involve you.' He looked at her intently. 'Promise me you won't even think about it. I don't want you in any sort of danger. I'd never forgive myself.'

Shocked by the intensity of his words, and the look in his eyes, Nanette could only whisper, 'I promise, JC,' as the waiter arrived with their meal.

The news of Zac's victory in the British Grand Prix was on the car radio late Sunday afternoon as they returned to Monaco.

'It is possible he makes champion this year,' Jean-Claude said thoughtfully. 'He's driving really well.'

Nanette nodded.

'He'll be on a real high when he gets back on Tuesday,' she said. 'Making him accept no for an answer to his proposal will be difficult.'

'Would you like me to tell him for you?' Jean-Claude asked.

Nanette smiled at him gratefully.

'Thanks for the offer but I think it's something I must do myself.'

As Jean-Claude stopped the car outside the apartment, Nanette leant across and kissed him gently on the cheek.

'I've really enjoyed today, JC. Thank you.'

Jean-Claude looked at her steadily before unexpectedly placing his arm around her shoulders and pulling her towards him. His kiss was gentle and undemanding and a surprised Nanette was totally unprepared for the emotions it unleashed within her.

As they drew apart she stared at him.

'I'll see you tomorrow,' Jean-Claude said, eventually releasing her. Wordlessly Nanette got out and closed the car door. Jean-Claude gave her an enigmatic smile before turning the steering wheel and driving away.

Nanette, her thoughts in turmoil, watched as the car disappeared. Had that kiss meant the same to him as it had to her? Or was she over-reacting to a gesture that was maybe just a gesture of loving friendship from an older man?

The following morning Mathieu left on his business trip and Nanette's day slipped into its normal routine imposed by the twin's school timetable.

With the memory of Jean-Claude's kiss fresh in her mind, Nanette felt strangely shy when she took the twins up to his villa for their routine after-school swim. But she needn't have worried. Jean-Claude, always the perfect gentleman, greeted her and the twins in his normal manner.

It was only when they were alone for a few minutes as the twins dried and dressed themselves, that he took her in his arms and gently kissed her.

'How are you today, *ma chérie*?' he asked. Nanette smiled at him shyly, as her heart skipped a beat at his use of the endearment. She hadn't imagined it; the kiss had meant something to him as well.

'Do you have any plans for tomorrow evening?' he asked. 'I thought maybe you'd like some company after the twins are in bed,' he added.

Realizing that Jean-Claude had remembered that tomorrow was the third anniversary of her accident, Nanette nodded.

'Please.'

'I have a business meeting early evening but I should be with you by about nine o'clock,' Jean-Claude said.

'The twins have a school play rehearsal. I have to collect them at eight-thirty so by the time we've walked back that would be perfect.'

'Good. I think we have things to talk about, *ma chérie*.' Jean-Claude said softly.

The streets were quiet as Nanette walked slowly through Monaco to collect the twins the following evening. It would be another half-hour before the rush of people out to enjoy themselves for the evening began to make their way to the restaurants and nightclubs.

The hall where the twins were rehearsing was part of the

modern apartment block where Zac had lived years ago and Nanette found her footsteps dragging the nearer she got to the building.

Having deliberately avoided this particular area of Monte Carlo since her return, Nanette couldn't help thinking how ironic it was that it should be this evening of all evenings that she was once again having to come to this particular building.

Nanette tried to push thoughts of the past out of her mind and concentrate on present-day aspects of her life – the twins, Jean-Claude, particularly Jean-Claude – but as she crossed the road towards the apartment block, images from her past began to merge with the present-day ones.

The lights were on in various apartments, including No.5 where she and Zac had spent so much time together. As Nanette glanced up, a glamorous woman came to the window, drawing the curtains, shutting Nanette and the world out.

Standing in the middle of the small service road that led to the underground garage, Nanette stared up at the window. Three years ago she and Zac were in that apartment getting ready to go out and celebrate her birthday before he left for the next Grand Prix.

She remembered how happy she'd been as they left the apartment. Stepping hand in hand with Zac into the lift to go down to the garage. Walking across to her new car and driving slowly up out of the underground exit, making for the auto route and their dinner reservation in Mougins.

The start of what had been a perfect evening with the man she loved – and whom she'd thought loved her.

An unexpected shiver racked her body and Nanette took several deep breaths trying to regain her composure. But images from later on that fateful evening were beginning to crowd into her brain.

Things she'd forgotten until now. The champagne they'd drunk, the friends they'd met up with, the rain that had begun to fall as they left the restaurant. Zac's insistence—

Nanette jumped as a car horn blared out behind her.

'Hey, lady, that's not the best place to stand – unless you want to be run down.' The man in the expensive sports car leant out of his window and rebuked her.

Nanette smiled weakly and mouthed the word 'sorry' in his direction, before moving back on to the narrow pavement, and allowing the man and his car to disappear down the ramp into the depths of the underground garage.

Shaking, she leant against the wall. It was several minutes before she felt strong enough to walk the few remaining yards to the rehearsal hall entrance.

It seemed only a matter of minutes before the twins ran out to join her.

'Hi, Netty,' Olivia said, taking hold of her hand as they began to walk, while Pierre ambled along in front.

'I didn't forget a single line tonight,' Olivia said proudly.

'Well done you,' Nanette said, struggling to talk normally. 'And you, Pierre? How did you get on?'

'OK,' Pierre said, turning round to look at her. 'I've only got three lines to say anyway. Are you all right? You don't look very well.'

'I've got a bit of a headache,' was the only thing she could think of saying. 'Come on, let's go home. Shall we have some hot chocolate when we get back?'

Once Nanette had seen the twins into bed she went through to the balcony and looked down at the boats bobbing around on their moorings.

Lights were shining out from the main cabin on *Pole Position* and as Nanette watched, a crew member came out on deck to check the position of the gangplank. Zac would be arriving on the late flight tonight and the crew knew better than not to have everything just right.

She stared down at the yacht, wondering why her memory had suddenly started to throw pictures of the past at her. Zac's proposition? Or maybe driving on Sunday had been the trigger? Whatever the catalyst, there appeared to be no stopping the flood of painful reminiscences that were crowding into her mind.

Large droplets of rain blew in unexpectedly under the shelter of the balcony and Nanette grimaced to herself. She gripped the balcony rail tightly as yet another vignette of that evening three years ago flooded into her consciousness.

The rain had started as they left the restaurant. By the time they were on the autoroute and heading for the first tunnel, it was torrential and Nanette expected Zac to decree leaving at the next exit. Instead he simply pressed the play button on the radio and the nostalgic words of 'Yesterday' struggled to be heard against the noise of the storm and the rhythmic sweep of windscreen wipers rendered useless by the force of the rain.

As they exited the tunnel, Nanette saw the huge sheet of water that lay in front of them a split second before the car rose up and aquaplaned out of control across this unexpected lake towards the central reservation. The impact jarred every bone in her body and turned the car over, sending it spinning on its roof back across to the hard shoulder where it finally came to rest.

Drifting in and out of consciousness Nanette was dimly aware of the nauseous smell of petrol and of Zac dragging her out and away from the wreckage.

'I've phoned for help. Shouldn't be too long,' Zac assured her as she lay on the verge.

The paramedics were kind and gently placed her on a stretcher. As they lifted her into the ambulance, Zac leant over her and whispered something.

Now, three years later, Nanette finally remembered what those words were.

'Nanette, I'm so sorry. Please forgive me.'

CHAPTER SEVEN

Nanette jumped as Jean-Claude appeared unexpectedly on the balcony. Lost in her memories she hadn't heard the apartment door opening.

'Is everything all right? You look very pale,' Jean-Claude said, holding her tight as he gave her a greeting kiss on the cheeks.

'Zac is due back soon. I was trying to work out what I'm going to say to him.'

'How about a straightforward, No thank you. I don't want the job with *Vacances au Soleil*.'

'It's no longer as simple as that, JC,' Nanette said quietly. 'I also need to talk to him about' – she took a deep breath before continuing – 'about the things I've started to remember.'

'Your memory of the accident is returning?'

Nanette nodded. 'Yes. Something triggered it off tonight as I walked past Zac's old apartment,' she said, beginning to shiver. 'And then when I came out here. . . .' Her voice trailed away as she gestured towards *Pole Position*.

Jean-Claude pulled her back into his arms protectively.

'These memories have clearly upset you. Do you wish to tell me?'

Standing in the safe circle of his arms, looking up at Jean-Claude's concerned face, Nanette wished she could confide in him. Ask his advice about how to approach things with Zac, but slowly she shook her head.

'I think I must talk to Zac first – see if my memory is true or whether it's playing tricks on me.'

Jean-Claude kissed her gently. '*D'accord*. You tell me when you're ready to talk about the past. Tonight we'll talk about us and perhaps the future.'

Nanette smiled at him gratefully as he took her hand and together they left the balcony. Nanette moved away from him to close the balcony doors and draw the heavy curtains across, but was startled by a loud knock on the apartment door.

'Ah supper,' Jean-Claude said. 'I'll get it. I missed dinner this evening because of my business appointment,' he explained, returning with several steaming containers which he placed on the dining table.

'I hope you like Chinese?'

Nanette organized the table, while Jean-Claude deftly turned out lights, lit candles, switched on the CD player and opened a bottle of wine. A few simple actions but Nanette realized that Jean-Claude had somehow introduced an atmosphere of intimacy into the room. Suddenly she felt shy and self-conscious. What was he expecting from her?

As the voice of Charles Aznavour singing a string of romantic melodies floated through the apartment, Jean-Claude turned to her.

'*Voilà*! Let's eat,' and gallantly he pulled a chair out for her.

The sweet and sour pork was delicious and Nanette was surprised to find how hungry she was. It wasn't until Jean-

Claude was pouring some wine that he glanced over and asked, 'Has Mathieu ever said anything to you about his mother? Or about me for that matter?'

Startled Nanette shook her head. 'No.'

'Before we talk about the future, I think I need to tell you a little about my past,' he said replacing the bottle in the terracotta wine cooler. 'Amelia and I were childhood sweethearts – our birthdays were just two days apart. I was the youngest – a fact which always amused her. Neither of our families thought we were good enough for each other.' Jean-Claude grinned ruefully. 'But when she became pregnant they became united in demanding we get married. Mathieu was born on Amelia's seventeenth birthday.'

He took a sip of his wine.

'At first everything was fine but when Amelia's family decided to move to Paris she thought we should go with them. I was all set to work in the family business and didn't want to move. In the end she decided she wanted to go with them – with or without me – but taking Mathieu.'

'That must have been hard for you to deal with,' Nanette said quietly.

'*Oui*. I don't think Mathieu has ever forgiven me. Looking back I think maybe I should have gone to Paris with them, that things could have been different.' Jean-Claude shook his head. 'One makes mistakes in life – particularly when one is so young.

'I visited as often as I could and we had some good times together but our lives were soon going in different directions.' He sighed. 'How could it do anything else? I was taking more and more responsibility for the family business and Amelia, well, let's just say Amelia was enjoying her life in Paris.'

There was a short silence as he swirled the wine in his glass.

'Mathieu was thirteen when Amelia was killed in a car crash and he came to live with me down here. Until all this blew up I thought I'd made a good job of raising him. We had a small problem with a car and some credit when he was a teenager, but on the whole he seemed to have become a well-adjusted, caring individual and I was proud of him. We had a good relationship. But now I just don't understand him at all.' Jean-Claude shook his head.

'JC, I'm sure things will work out for Mathieu. Like you I don't think he is inherently bad – he's just got caught up in something that's spiralled out of control.' She hesitated before asking, 'Has your detective uncovered anything?'

'Only the fact that Boris appears to be the one pulling all the strings. Apparently the police, both here and Interpol, are quietly keeping tabs on him. Unofficially the rumours are flying. There's talk of money-laundering, a business cartel and drugs being involved.'

'Mathieu wouldn't do drugs,' Nanette said instantly. 'It has to be something else. What about Zac? Has the detective figured out where he fits into all this?'

'*Non.* Other than that he seems to be pulling some strings of his own, independent of Boris. Who, incidentally, is currently in South America overseeing some business deal.'

'I wonder if that's where Mathieu is, too, this week. He didn't say where he was going. Just said it was a business trip,' Nanette said.

Jean-Claude shrugged. 'Mathieu caught a flight to London, but he could have picked up a connection to literally anywhere in the world from there. He hasn't rung to speak to the twins?'

'He e-mails them most days but only phones occasionally when he's away. I know he's promised to be back in time for their school play next week.'

'Good. Somehow I feel easier when he's in town – if anything happens here in the Principality at least I'll be around to help to sort it out.'

Jean-Claude gazed at Nanette thoughtfully. 'I wanted you to understand that, although it all went wrong, I did love Amelia.' He reached across and took her hand in his. 'And until now, I've never come close to loving anyone else.'

There was silence as Jean-Claude gently stroked Nanette's hand before looking up and asking quietly, 'Do you think you could ever look on me as more than a friend?'

Nanette's smile was warm as she smiled at him.

'Oh, JC, you're more than just a friend already.'

Before she could say any more the telephone rang. As she went to answer it, he sighed and began to clear the table. Nanette was still talking on the phone when he finished and he took the rest of his wine out on to the balcony to wait for her.

Nanette was smiling when she joined him a few minutes later.

'That was Patsy. Bryan has treated her to a flight out here – she's coming for my birthday! She wanted to know if I could meet her at Nice Airport. I said yes, of course, but I don't have a car. Could you possibly take me?'

'Of course.'

He placed an arm around her shoulders. 'Nanette, I meant what I said earlier about not loving anyone since Amelia. I know Zac hurt you very badly and I don't want to rush you into a relationship before you're sure, but do you think we could have any sort of future together?'

Nanette turned and kissed him gently. 'JC, I can't promise anything. Could we carry on as we are? Take things slowly, get to know each other properly – see what happens? Now my memory seems to be returning, there are a few things I'd like to sort out. I need to finally close the Zac Ewart part of my life.'

She didn't add the words, 'before I can love anyone again' but she hoped Jean-Claude understood.

The following morning, once she'd taken the twins to school, Nanette walked slowly along the embankment towards the Old Port. The envelope containing the *Vacances au Soleil* papers was in her bag ready to hand back to Zac. She was determined, too, that this time he would accept the fact that she didn't want the job he was offering her.

The crew on board *Pole Position* were busy with routine morning chores but there was no sign of Zac. As Nanette hesitated on the quay, the yacht's captain came down the gangway.

Recognizing her, he said, 'Zac's been delayed – something to do with the wrong tyres being supplied for Canada. There's a chance he'll not make it back here until after Indianapolis.'

'But that's a month away,' Nanette said. 'I need to talk to him before then.'

'I can give you his mobile number if that helps,' the captain said.

About to refuse the offer, Nanette changed her mind, saying instead, 'Thanks. That could be useful.'

Handing her a card with Zac's mobile number on it the skipper said, 'I'm surprised you don't already have this – particularly as you're coming back to work for Zac.'

'Who told you that?'

'Zac did before he left for the UK.'

Inwardly furious but not wanting to discuss it with the yacht skipper Nanette said simply, 'Oh, I see. Thanks for the number. See you around.'

Stopping at the first pavement café she reached, Nanette ordered a cappuccino. Her hand was shaking as she spooned the froth off the top and she took several deep breaths trying to steady her nerves.

Zac was unbelievable. Back to his old tricks of assuming he could browbeat her in to doing what he wanted. How dare he tell his crew that she would be working for him again, especially as she'd already told him she wasn't interested?

Opening her bag she took out the envelope to slip the card inside with the other papers. Tempting though it was to ring him, Nanette was determined to confront him face to face even if she had to wait another month to do it.

A shadow fell across the table and Nanette looked up in surprise.

'*Bonjour, Nanette.*' Mathieu sat down beside her. 'Join me for another coffee?'

Nanette shook her head. 'No thanks. What are you doing here? We weren't expecting you back until at least the weekend.'

He shrugged. 'A couple of my business appointments were cancelled so I decided to come home early. How are the twins? Still practising for their concert?'

'Yes. They'll be pleased to see you.'

'I'll meet them from school this afternoon if you like,' Mathieu offered. He took a sip of coffee before asking, 'Spoken to Zac recently?'

Nanette shook her head. 'I was hoping to see him today, to sort some things out, but he's not here.'

'I know,' Mathieu said quietly. 'I was supposed to be meeting up with him in the UK but he had to take an early flight to Canada.'

He glanced at her. 'Do you still have the papers he gave you about *Vacances au Soleil*?'

'Yes. They're in my bag. I was going to give them back this morning.'

'Could I have a look at them please?'

'Oh, Mathieu, I don't know,' Nanette protested.

'Are they marked private and confidential? Did Zac ask you to keep them to yourself?' Mathieu pressed her.

'No.'

'There may just be something in them that would help me,' Mathieu said quietly.

'Help you do what? It's only papers outlining Zac's business and what I would be expected to do.'

Mathieu was silent for a few seconds. 'I need a certain piece of information and there's a possibility it will be in those papers. Please, Nanette. I promise you Zac will never know you showed them to me.'

Nanette stood up. 'Mathieu, I'm not happy doing this, but I will let you see them, only not here. Back at the apartment.'

'That stuff tastes vile,' Ralph said, as Vanessa handed him some diluted Sangre de Grado to swallow. 'Do I have to?'

Vanessa nodded. 'Yes, you do. And I need to rub some of

the ointment onto the last of your bruises too.'

Three days after his accident and to Vanessa's relief, Ralph was a lot better. Whether it was the smelly concoctions that the head shaman had given her to administer on a regular basis or whether he hadn't been as badly injured as at first feared, Vanessa didn't know. She was just relieved he was alive.

'I don't know what's in this stuff,' Vanessa said, as she rubbed the reddish sticky ointment into Ralph's body, 'but it's certainly worked.'

'Seems to take the pain away too,' Ralph said. 'Can't believe that something so primitive has such great healing properties.'

'Don't forget the TLC I've given you will have made a difference too,' Vanessa teased.

Ralph caught hold of her hand. 'I know,' he said seriously. 'I'm sorry things haven't worked out as we planned. Nick and Harry were in here earlier saying that as they can't do any filming near the dam, they've persuaded Luigi to take them to film the young pink dolphins for a couple of days. I know it's a long trek but why don't you go to?'

Vanessa shook her head. 'Rather be here with you. Besides, I've promised Angela I'll help her and the other women this afternoon.'

'If you're sure. With a bit of luck we might see some dolphins on our trek northwards when we finally leave here anyway. Ah, here comes Matron and the consultant doing their rounds,' he added *sotto voce* as Angela and the head shaman appeared at the entrance to the hut.

After the medicine man had pronounced himself happy with Ralph's progress he said something urgently to Angela before leaving.

'He says you can get up today,' Angela said. 'There will be a feast in the village tomorrow night to celebrate your recovery.'

Early that afternoon Vanessa left Ralph writing in his journal and reviewing the plans for the next part of their adventure. Making her way towards the hut where the women were working at the far end of the village compound, she listened to the now familiar exotic chorus of birdsong from high in the surrounding trees.

She stopped to watch a crowd of yellow crowned Amazon parrots squawking and bickering over some spilled seeds whilst the village pig rooted in some undergrowth just yards away. The small monkey who'd taken her banana the very first day they'd arrived in the village ran towards her chattering excitedly, weaving in and out of her legs as she approached the hut.

Angela was busy sorting through a haphazard pile of muddy boots and dangerous looking machetes and smiled her welcome at Vanessa.

Standing in the entrance of the hut, Vanessa watched as several of the village women began sorting through the remains of the Brazil nut harvest. She was surprised by how few nuts there were.

'We have to sell most of the harvest,' Angela explained. 'And this year was not very productive. I hope next year will be better but then the *aviamento* will have changed too.' She shrugged. 'We know already we will be paying a higher price before the next harvest.'

Vanessa looked at her questioningly. '*Aviamento*?'

'It's the system that provides these,' Angela said,

gesticulating towards the boots and machetes.

'We get the stuff necessary to do the harvesting on the understanding that this middle man will buy the nuts from us at a low price. He will sell them on and take any profit we should have had.'

'That's terrible. Can't you sell the nuts direct?'

'No. We need the equipment to gather them and don't have the money to buy it.'

'The government farm where you got the seedlings from – can't they help?'

Angela shook her head. 'In the past they talked about helping us to change the system but nothing happened. And now this foreign guy's man from Rio has muscled in on the nuts as well as the dam.' She glanced up. 'Luigi thinks we'll end up being forced to leave. We don't need a lot of money to survive here but we do need land and food. Brazil nuts give us both our flour and oil.'

'Is there enough there for the villagers until the next harvest?' Vanessa asked.

Angela shrugged. 'Depends on how well they keep. It's difficult to stop them going mouldy in this humidity as we don't have proper storage.'

There was a short silence as both women looked around, each lost in their own thoughts.

It was Vanessa who broke the silence. 'Do you want a hand cleaning those machetes then? Or is there something else you want me to do?'

'Be careful how you handle them,' was all Angela said, as she handed her a piece of rag.

As she carefully cleaned the lethal tools, Vanessa couldn't stop thinking about the problems the villagers faced. There had to be an answer.

Ambling back through the compound after the work was finished, Vanessa found Ralph waiting for her outside the large communal hut.

'You don't look very happy,' he said, taking her hand as they walked towards their own hut.

Vanessa sighed. 'I just feel so sad for this place. Everyone knows the rain forest is dying because of the way agriculture is taking over, but the people are dying too – if not physically, by being forced to move out of their villages. Give up their traditional way of life. Even Angela is talking of leaving.'

Ralph was silent as a frustrated Vanessa aimlessly scuffed up some earth with her foot.

'I'm hoping my film will make people sit up and take notice. Do something about the problems,' he said quietly.

'I know you came to film the true story of the natives,' she said squeezing his hand.

'I just hope it isn't too late and it just serves as archive material for the way it all was.'

There was a short pause before Vanessa deliberately changed the subject. 'How are you feeling? It's lovely to have you up and about again, but you mustn't overdo it. I must ask Angela to show me how to make that ointment before we leave and take some home with us. The twins are always falling over getting bruises and. . . .' She stopped in her tracks and pulled Ralph round to face her.

'That's it,' she said excitedly.

'What?'

'I've thought of something we *can* do to help the villagers and preserve their way of life. We'll help them form a co-operative to sell their natural remedies and their produce including the Brazil nuts. With a co-operative at least the villagers will be in control themselves and not some sleazy middle man.'

It was late in the afternoon of Nanette's birthday and she and Patsy were out on the balcony of Mathieu's apartment arranging a magnificent bouquet of flowers from Jean-Claude.

They'd spent the day mooching around Monaco old town and entertaining the twins before returning to the apartment. Mathieu had now taken Olivia and Pierre off swimming and the sisters were finally catching up on each other's news.

'These are beautiful flowers,' Patsy said. 'Jean-Claude must be really fond of you,' she added with a sideways look at her sister.

'It was so good of Bryan to treat you to this holiday,' Nanette said, not rising to the bait. 'Shame he couldn't come with you.'

'Wrong time of year for a farmer to take a holiday,' Patsy said ruefully. 'What with silage and haymaking, not to mention baby calves arriving. I'm sure Helen is enjoying looking after him though.'

'Getting in practice for the new arrival?' Nanette teased.

Patsy groaned. 'Don't. I'm really quite fond of her and I know she's excited at becoming a grandmother, but she does have this tendency to try and take over.' She glanced at Nanette. 'You will still be able to come back and be with me when "the bump" makes its appearance? I'll understand if you can't though.'

'I'm going to do my best,' Nanette answered. 'It all depends.' She paused and concentrated on carefully pushing the last orchid into the arrangement. 'I may end up bringing the twins with me.'

Patsy gave her sister a quizzical look. 'I get the feeling something is clearly going on down here – and not just with Jean-Claude either. Tell me all!'

Nanette blushed, but decided to ignore her sister's remark about Jean-Claude for the moment.

'We think, no, we know, Mathieu and Zac are embroiled in something illegal. And can you believe Zac wants me to work for him again?'

'I hope you've told him no way!'

'I tried to, but he wasn't listening to me. And now Mathieu says it would help him if I did.' Nanette shrugged helplessly. 'But JC is against it, even to help Mathieu.'

'Does Vanessa know about your worries over Mathieu?'

Nanette shook her head. 'No. She's too far away to do anything and I don't want to worry her unless I have to.' Nanette glanced across at her sister. 'There's another thing. I'm starting to remember things about the accident.'

'That's good,' Patsy said. 'Isn't it?'

'Not sure. Yes, it's good that my memory is fully functional again but some of the things I'm remembering are frightening.'

'Not started the nightmares again?'

'No.'

'That's all right then.' Patsy said comfortably. 'Now, I'm sure this Mathieu business will eventually sort itself out and anyway, there's nothing you can do about it. What I really want to know about is you and Jean-Claude. He's very attractive.'

Before Nanette could answer, Florence, the housekeeper,

appeared with another large bunch of flowers.

'The concierge just sent these up, with this card,' she said, handing an envelope to Nanette.

Even before she tore open the envelope, Nanette knew who these particular flowers were from.

Happy Birthday. Sorry about missing our dinner date. Will ring you this evening. Hope you've had a great day. Zac.

Exasperated, Nanette said. 'They're lovely flowers but I wish he hadn't sent them. I'm going to have to say thank you and the last thing I want to do at the moment is thank Zac Ewart for anything. And why is he going to ring me this evening?'

'We won't be here anyway, will we?' Patsy said. 'Aren't we going out to dinner in' – she looked at her watch – 'about an hour, with Jean-Claude and Mathieu to celebrate your birthday in style?'

'Heavens, is it that late already? We'd better get ready.' Nanette took Zac's flowers out to the kitchen and asked Florence if she'd kindly find a vase for them.

Mathieu, arriving back with the twins from swimming just then, handed Nanette a small package.

'Olivia and Pierre thought you'd like this. Happy Birthday from us all.'

'This' turned out to be a beautiful silk scarf from one of the designer boutiques on Avenue de Monte Carlo.

'Thank you,' Nanette said, gently fingering the luxurious material. 'It's lovely. I shall wear it this evening.'

The Italian restaurant where Jean-Claude had booked a table was only a short walk away. Nanette's heart missed a beat as she saw him standing there waiting for them.

'Happy birthday,' he said in greeting. The words *ma chérie* were added so quietly, that only Nanette heard them and she smiled at him gratefully. Gallantly taking her hand in his, Jean-Claude escorted her to their table where an attentive waiter was waiting to pour the champagne before taking their orders.

A pianist was playing a medley of Italian songs and several couples were making use of the small dance floor around which the tables were grouped.

'Will you excuse us while the birthday girl and I have this dance?' Jean-Claude asked, looking at Mathieu and Patsy.

'Go ahead,' Mathieu said looking at Patsy. 'Would you like to?'

'I'll sit this one out, thanks,' Patsy answered. 'I think the bump would rather get in the way.'

Nanette, moving slowly around the dance-floor, Jean-Claude's arms holding her close, breathed a sigh of happiness. A feeling that this birthday was going to herald in a year of changes to her life flooded through her body – and surely this time, they would be good changes.

'Thank you for my beautiful flowers, JC,' Nanette murmured.

'My pleasure. I have another present for you, too, but you will have to come to the villa to collect it. Maybe when Patsy has returned home? Now we'd better return to our table, I can see the waiters arriving with our food.'

The meal was delicious. Conversation and laughter flowed between the four of them. It was only when the waiter brought the sweet trolley for them to choose from that she realized Patsy had gone quiet.

Concerned she looked at her.

'Patsy are you all right? You look awfully pale.'

'I'm fine – just feel a bit queasy. Probably too much rich food. I think I'll skip dessert.'

'Do you want to go home?' Nanette asked.

'Certainly not. But if you could just point me in the direction of the ladies?'

'I'll come with you,' Nanette said, giving her an anxious look.

'You stay here,' Patsy said standing up. 'I'm pregnant – not incapacitated. I see they've got your favourite dessert,' she added glancing at the trolley. 'So enjoy.'

But Nanette could hardly swallow a spoonful of her tiramisu, delicious as it was. When after ten minutes Patsy hadn't returned she stood up.

'I'll just go check on Patsy,' she said.

Nanette found her sister, sitting in a wicker chair, sipping a glass of water given to her by the concerned restroom attendant.

'What's going on?'

'The doctor should be here any minute,' the attendant answered. 'I've told the lady not to move.'

'Why do you need a doctor?' Nanette demanded. 'Is it the baby?'

Patsy bit her lip. 'I've started to bleed. Not a lot,' she added quickly seeing Nanette's face. 'But enough for me to need some medical advice.'

The restroom door swung open and a man entered.

'I'm the emergency doctor. I gather we have a problem with a pregnant lady? Perhaps I could ask everyone to wait outside for a while?'

'Doctor, my sister doesn't speak French,' Nanette said. 'Do you need me to translate?'

'*Non, merci.* I speak enough English. Please give me five minutes alone with the patient.'

Nanette made her way back to Jean-Claude and Mathieu and quickly explained the situation to them, before returning to see what the doctor said.

'Bed rest for the next twenty-four hours. And then check with a doctor again. No exertion.'

'How about flying? I'm booked to return to the UK in a couple of days?' Patsy asked.

The doctor shrugged his shoulders. 'Go to the clinic and see what the consultant advises.'

Jean-Claude insisted on calling a taxi to return to the apartment where he and Mathieu solicitously helped Patsy across the foyer to the lift. Once back in the apartment, Nanette saw Patsy into her room before joining the men in the sitting-room.

Mathieu was holding a piece of paper which he handed to Nanette.

'Florence left this note for you. Apparently Zac has been ringing all evening.'

Nanette sighed as she read the housekeeper's message:

Zac Ewart needs to talk to you urgently. Would you please ring him at whatever time you return. Mathieu will give you the number if you don't have it.

'What on earth can be so important? I'll ring him in the morning,' Nanette said. 'I'm too tired and worried about Patsy right now.'

As Mathieu went to say something, Nanette held up her hands.

'Mathieu, my days of running after Zac are long gone. Incidentally have you finished with the *Vacances au Soleil* papers yet?'

Jean-Claude shot his son a swift glance. 'What were you hoping to find?'

Mathieu shrugged. 'Just an address.'

'And was it there?' Jean-Claude asked.

There was a barely perceptible pause before Mathieu shook his head. 'No. I'll get the papers for you now,' He went into his temporary office, returning seconds later with Nanette's envelope.

'I said I'd take Patsy in some warm milk to help her sleep,' Nanette said. 'Shall I make us a nightcap too?'

Mathieu shook his head. 'Not for me. I've got a breakfast business meeting tomorrow so, if you'll excuse me, I'm off to bed. Goodnight.'

Nanette said to Jean-Claude as the door closed behind Mathieu, 'Can I get you anything?'

'No thanks. I'll leave you to look after Patsy – and don't worry. I'm sure she and the baby will be fine. I'll see you tomorrow.'

'Thank you for a lovely evening, JC,' Nanette said. 'I really enjoyed myself.'

Jean-Claude gave her a gentle kiss and he was gone.

As the door closed behind him, the telephone rang. Quickly Nanette snatched the receiver off its hook before the shrill noise could disturb everyone.

'Zac stop pestering me—'

'I need your help, Nanette,' Zac's voice interrupted. 'I want you to go to *Pole Position*, meet someone and put something in the safe for me.'

'What? You ring at nearly midnight to ask me to do something trivial that your skipper can do?' Nanette said incredulously.

'No, he can't,' Zac answered quietly. 'You're the only person apart from me who knows a) where the safe is and b) the combination to it.'

'You mean the secret, personal one, in your cabin?' Nanette asked, as realization dawned. 'You've never changed the code?'

'No.'

'Can't the skipper simply put whatever it is, in the main safe until you get back?'

Zac sighed audibly down the phone. 'If I hadn't had to come out here early there wouldn't be a problem – I'd have been there to deal with it myself. As it is, I'm unlikely to get back for a few weeks. I'd rather it was totally out of sight. Five minutes, Nanette, that's all it will take.'

'You're not asking me to help with something illegal are you?' Nanette demanded.

'Definitely not,' Zac replied instantly. 'If it makes you feel any better I can tell you it's something to do with *Vacances au Soleil*.'

Nanette took a deep breath.

'OK,' she said reluctantly. 'I'll do it tomorrow.'

'Good. Eleven o'clock on board. You do remember the combination?'

'Yes.'

'Thanks, Nanette. I owe you one.'

'If my returning memory is right, Zac, you owe me more

than that,' Nanette said.

'When you get back we need to have a serious talk. Goodnight.'

Quickly, before Zac could start to question her, Nanette replaced the receiver. She was determined to challenge Zac face to face, to see his reaction to her accusation. Now was not the time.

Tomorrow she would go to the yacht and do as Zac asked – but this was positively the last time she would do anything Zac Ewart asked of her.

CHAPTER EIGHT

The next morning Nanette took the twins to school before returning to the apartment and making Patsy some breakfast.

'You still look a bit peaky,' Nanette said. 'How do you feel?'

'OK, thanks, and I'm really sorry for spoiling your evening,' Patsy said. 'Did I hear the phone last night, after Jean-Claude had left?'

Nanette nodded. 'Zac.'

Patsy looked at her. 'And?'

'I'm going to collect something and put it in his personal safe on board *Pole Position* this morning,' Nanette answered slowly, knowing that Patsy wouldn't like it. 'Don't worry,' she added. 'It's not good for you in your condition. It'll only take five minutes and then I intend to forget about Zac Ewart until he gets back from Indianapolis next month.'

'Do you know what it is you're collecting?' Patsy asked.

'No. But it can't be anything too large because the safe isn't that big,' she answered.

'Have you told Jean-Claude or Mathieu what you're doing?'

Nanette shook her head. 'No. Mathieu has already left and I'm not expecting to see Jean-Claude this morning.

'What are you doing?' This, as Patsy went to throw off the bedcovers.

'I'm getting up and coming with you,' Patsy said.

'Oh no you're not. The doctor said bed rest for twenty-four hours, so don't you even dare to think about getting up,' Nanette scolded her. 'And when I get back I'm ringing the clinic to make you an appointment for tomorrow,' she said and tucked Patsy firmly back into bed.

Later that morning she left Patsy with some magazines and strict instructions to take it easy and made her way down to the harbour.

Walking towards the yacht she could see the gangplank was raised making access from the quay impossible. Hadn't Zac told the crew he'd arranged for her to meet someone on board? What would she do if the crew had all disappeared for the day and she couldn't get on board?

To her relief as she got nearer, she saw Phil, the skipper, out on the starboard deck talking to someone on the next yacht. Seeing her standing at the stern, Phil raised a hand in greeting but didn't immediately move to lower the gangplank and let her on board. Instead, he finished his conversation and took his time before pressing the button that would lower the gangplank. Nanette was sure he would never have dared to have kept Zac waiting, but he was clearly trying to make a point.

'Zac has asked me to meet someone here and—'

'I know,' Phil interrupted. 'He phoned me this morning.' He looked hard at her. 'I'm sure you are aware that the captain of a boat is the one held legally responsible for whatever takes place on board – regardless of whether he or the owner sanctioned it.'

'Yes, I know,' Nanette said quietly. 'All I can say is, Zac assured me last night, that it is nothing illegal he wants me to put in the safe, otherwise I certainly wouldn't be here.'

'Until this morning I wasn't even aware there was a second *secret* safe on board this yacht. It is something I should have been told about.'

'This is something you are going to have to take up with him.'

'Oh, I intend to,' Phil said. 'But if you speak to him before I do, you can tell him that I'm seriously thinking of looking for another position – one where the owner treats me with the respect and trust I deserve.'

Nanette was silent, not knowing what to say.

'Cooee.'

They both turned to see Evie standing on the quay.

'Hi, Nanette, haven't seen you in ages. How are you? Can I come on board?'

Without waiting for a reply Evie slipped off her high heels and walked down the gangplank.

'I've got a package for Zac,' she said, rummaging in her bag and producing a paperback-sized parcel.

'You have?' Nanette said surprised. The last person she'd expected to be meeting was Evie.

'It's from Luc,' Evie explained. 'My ex-boss as of today,' and she held the package out to Phil.

Phil shook his head, declining to accept the parcel. 'Not me. Nanette is here to collect it – and put it somewhere safe,' he added.

Evie looked at the two of them, clearly sensing the tension, before shrugging her shoulders. 'Whatever. I've done my bit.'

'Thanks,' Nanette said, taking the parcel.

'Have you got time for a coffee?' Evie asked.

'Love one. Give me five minutes to put this away first.'

'All right if I go down below?' Nanette asked, turning to Phil.

'Be my guest – you know where it is,' and Phil moved away indifferently.

Closing the master cabin door behind her, Nanette walked across the cream deep-pile carpet towards the en-suite bathroom.

The luxurious bathroom with its marble and gold fittings had been spared refurbishment last year and was exactly as Nanette remembered it. Kneeling down she opened the vanity unit under the double marble sink and lifted out the white towels that were stored there.

Carefully she tapped at the front edge of the flooring shelf to loosen it before lifting it out and laying it on the floor. Sitting back on her heels she looked at the small dial previously hidden by the false cupboard bottom but now exposed in the recess under the sink. What was she going to find when the safe door opened? What secrets did Zac already have stashed away within the steel box?

Nanette took a deep breath. It had been a long time since she and Zac had devised the code. She only hoped she could remember it.

Counting under her breath, and slowly turning the dial, Nanette concentrated on remembering the correct sequence of numbers and the number of turns she had to make to the right and then to the left before she heard the satisfying *click* of the lock undoing and she was able to pull open the door.

The safe was empty – except for the handgun. Nanette stared at it stunned. Since when had Zac found it necessary to have a gun on board? Sitting back on her heels Nanette looked at the packet Evie had given her, wondering about its contents. She sat there for several minutes before coming to a decision and closing the door and spinning the combination lock.

The flooring shelf slid back in easily and Nanette replaced the towels tidily before shutting the vanity unit door, picking up her handbag and leaving the bathroom.

Evie was waiting for her in the stern and Nanette quickly said 'Goodbye' to Phil who was busy adjusting fenders near the bow, before following Evie down the gangplank and back on to the quay.

'Shall we have coffee at the apartment?' Nanette suggested. 'Then I can introduce you to my sister Patsy. And, tell me, why is Luc your ex-boss?'

Evie sighed and glanced around before saying quietly, 'I think his business is in trouble. He's talking of restructuring, or he may give up altogether. Anyway, he's given me two months' pay in lieu of notice and told me he doesn't need me anymore. He has promised to help me find another job if I want to stay in Monaco. Which I do.'

'Have you heard of any jobs going?'

'No. But I've got an interview with an agency tomorrow so I'm hoping they'll come up with something,' Evie said. 'Even if it's only temporary.'

Nanette glanced at Evie as a sudden thought struck her. Should she tell her about Zac needing someone for *Vacances au Soleil*? But how could she possibly recommend a job with Zac when she suspected he was involved in something illegal?

Instead she said, 'I'll have a word with Jean-Claude if you like, he may know of something.'

'Thanks,' Evie said. 'I'm hoping something does turn up. I really like it down here and would hate to have to leave.'

The consultant at the clinic where Nanette had made an appointment for Patsy was thorough in his examination. And definite in his opinion.

'Everything seems fine now. But I suggest you fly home as soon as possible in case the bleeding starts again. Leave it too late and perhaps the airline will refuse to let you fly. I think you will possibly deliver early.'

Leaving the clinic the sisters decided to walk back to the apartment. As they strolled slowly along the embankment enjoying the sunshine and dodging the tourists, Nanette said, 'I'll ring the airline and change your ticket to an earlier flight. As much as I want you to stay, I think the consultant is right.'

Patsy nodded. 'Another twenty-four hours will be OK though, won't it? I really want to see the twins' school play tonight.'

'First available flight after this evening then,' Nanette said. 'Now, are you up for some retail therapy in Rue Princess Caroline before lunch?'

'Silly question, of course,' Patsy answered. 'I've got to make the most of my time here – besides I must find a present for Bryan.'

'Good, but then you must get some rest before we go to the play. It's my afternoon to work for Jean-Claude so I won't be around for a couple of hours. If you don't want to stay in the apartment alone you can always come up to the villa with me.'

Patsy shook her head. 'I'll be fine. I'll probably sit on the balcony and snooze for a couple of hours. Shopping always tires me out even when I'm not pregnant!'

Once back at the apartment Patsy went to sit on the balcony while Nanette telephoned the airline to change her flight. To her dismay she was told the only flight with seats available was just eight hours before the one Patsy was already booked on – hardly worth the cost of changing.

Nanette glanced at her sister dozing happily in one of the wicker chairs on the balcony and decided to simply abandon the idea of getting Patsy home early. She still had at least five weeks to go and Nanette began to pray that the consultant's possible early delivery prediction fears wouldn't be proved true in the next few days.

Bryan, she knew, would be devastated if he wasn't with Patsy when she gave birth to their first child. How she was going to keep her own promise to be with her sister was something she'd worry about next month.

In the afternoon, and leaving Patsy with strict instructions to rest until she returned, Nanette made her way up to Jean-Claude's villa.

He was waiting for her in the garden and Nanette's heart skipped a beat as she saw him. As much as she might tell herself not to rush things, she knew she was falling in love. Standing in the circle of his arms as he held her tightly, she felt herself tremble with desire as he kissed her.

Several moments passed before he released her with a sigh.

'How did the appointment with the consultant go?'

'Everything seems to be all right although he thinks Patsy should go home earlier but I can't change the flight – no seats available,' Nanette answered slowly. 'Haven't mentioned this to Patsy but now I'm worried that they'll refuse to take her anyway if we mention what's happened.'

'When does she want to go?'

'Tomorrow would have been ideal,' Nanette said.

'Excuse me a moment.' Jean-Claude punched some numbers into his mobile.

As he began to talk in rapid French, Nanette wandered across to the terrace wall and looked down on the Mediterranean sparkling under the azure blue sky. Jean-Claude joined her a few moments later.

'*Voilà*. Patsy flies tomorrow at fourteen hundred hours from Cannes-Mandelieu. I will drive you both there. You will arrange for her husband to meet her, yes?'

Nanette looked at him in amazement. 'How?'

'I have a friend with a private jet. He, like me, is happy to help,' Jean-Claude said. 'He flies to the UK several times a week on business and tomorrow he happens to have a spare seat.'

Nanette smiled. She'd forgotten how different the rich really were with their private planes and expensive habits. 'Thank you, JC.'

'Now, come with me,' Jean-Claude said. 'I want to give you your birthday presents,' and catching hold of her hand he led her towards the garage where he kept his Lotus.

'I'm sorry it's a day or two late but I wanted to show it to you in private,' he said, opening the door of a white convertible parked next to it. To Nanette's amazement he handed her the car keys.

'I know you aren't ready to start driving again yet, but I hope you will be soon. It will be here waiting for you.'

'JC, I don't know what to say.'

'You don't have to say anything. Just put the keys in your bag so you have them when you need them.'

Jean-Claude reached in the car and picked up a small orange drawstring bag that was on the driver's seat and handed it to her.

'But this is your real birthday present from me, *ma chérie*.'

Nanette was quiet as she opened the bag she recognizted as coming from the exclusive Hermes boutique near the Casino. Inside the bag itself was a padded, silk-lined box.

Nanette caught her breath as she lifted the lid and saw the watch nestling in the folds of silk.

'JC, thank you,' Nanette said, gazing in amazement at the watch with its diamond-studded case and bracelet. 'It's gorgeous. I've never been so spoilt. I'm overwhelmed.'

'Does the strap fit?' Jean-Claude asked anxiously. 'Let me help you put it on.'

Bent solicitously over her wrist, checking it fitted correctly, he said quietly, 'It's wonderful to have someone special to spoil,' before taking her in his arms and kissing her. As his lips claimed hers, Nanette abandoned herself to the delicious feelings swamping her body and returned his kiss passionately.

In the hours following Vanessa's idea of forming a co-operative to sell the village produce, she and Ralph discussed endlessly the kind of things they could do – things that they thought would make a real difference.

List after list littered the floor of their hut. Ralph wrote down the names of possible sponsors – people who owed him favours and would be happy to participate. Vanessa wrote down every product she could think of that could be sold and then both she and Ralph tried to look at the logistics of the whole thing. From producing, to harvesting, to storing, to marketing and – a major stumbling block – actually getting the stuff out of the jungle.

'We need to organize a meeting with the villagers,' Ralph said, 'before we get too carried away. Find out exactly how they would like things to work – if in fact they think it's a good idea.'

'You do think they'll go for it, don't you?' Vanessa asked anxiously. 'It's for their future, not ours.'

Ralph was silent for a moment.

'I'm not sure. Remember the warning I was given before my accident not to interfere? Not all the villagers like us, me, being here. This Rio guy seems to have the villagers agreeing to his boss's every move. You need to convince the head shaman that the villagers will benefit. It's all a matter of trust,' he added. 'They like you so hopefully they will trust you enough to work with you.' He glanced at her. 'You know what they call you don't you?'

Vanessa shook her head.

'*Pacchumama* – roughly translated it means Earth Mother. They love the way you are with the animals and the children.'

Vanessa smiled. 'Do they really? Maybe at the celebration tonight we can put our ideas to them and see if they've got any of their own,' Vanessa said. 'You're right – we do need to get them involved from the very beginning – if only to prove to them we don't have any ulterior motives.'

'You do realize just how much it is going to take to get this project off the ground?' Ralph replied. 'And to keep it running? I'm not just talking about money here – it's going to take a huge amount of time.'

'I know,' Vanessa said. 'But we've got to try.'

'I'll give you all the help I can but I'm already committed to other projects when we get back. I won't be around full time – a lot of the organizing will fall on you.'

'Organizing is something I'm good at,' Vanessa said. 'Right, tonight at the celebration party for your recovery, I'll talk to Angela and the others.'

But while Angela was openly enthusiastic, some of the other women were hostile to the idea and Vanessa found herself having to explain again and again how a co-operative would work to their advantage. And, no, she wouldn't personally benefit from it.

By the time she was sitting on the floor next to the head shaman outlining the way the villagers could protect their own futures, it was clear that opinion was divided.

'We have an agreement with the outsider,' said the head shaman, resplendent in his native dress and war paint. 'He is already helping with the gold mine and next year he has promised to help with equipment for the nut harvest. His Brazilian man is due here again soon to pay us for the gold we have mined, so we shall have money for necessary supplies.'

At his words, Vanessa felt her heart sank. 'You don't think. . . ?'

He held his hand up to stop her. 'We are people of our word. So, I thank you for your concerns, but we are already committed.'

Beside her, Angela said something quickly and the shaman answered with an emphatic shake of his head before he stood up and moved away.

'Is that it then?' Vanessa said turning to Angela.

Angela nodded. 'The men are sure this man will do more

and more to help us – besides, they are also aware of the dangers of upsetting him,' she added quietly.

'What about the women? They could do something themselves,' Vanessa said, trying to hide her disappointment.

Angela shook her head. 'The men would forbid it.'

Later that night when Vanessa and Ralph had returned to their hut and were preparing to climb into their hammocks she said sadly, 'I was really looking forward to organizing the co-op. I even had a name ready, "Fruits of the Forest".'

'Maybe it's for the best,' Ralph said, trying to comfort her. 'We'll be home in a few weeks. You'll have to put your organizational skills to work on marketing my film. Bring the plight of the jungle and its inhabitants to the world's attention that way.'

'Of course I'll do everything possible to publicize your film,' Vanessa said, 'but I wanted to do something, try to make a difference, myself. I still can't believe that they've turned the idea of a co-operative down because of some sleazy guy the head shaman has given his word to.'

'This outsider, as the shaman calls him, clearly thinks he's on to something sending his henchman from Rio all this way into the forest,' Ralph said thoughtfully. 'Wonder who he is?'

Vanessa shrugged and shook her head. 'We'll never know. I just wish the villagers could see that the co-operative would have given them so much more control over their own future – and that of the jungle,' she added.

For the next couple of days Ralph concentrated on getting as much filming done as possible, before they began their long trek back to civilization and then home. As their day of departure drew near, Vanessa found herself thinking more and more about the twins. Keeping in touch had proved impossible from so deep in the jungle and she was looking forward to reaching Manaus on the Amazon in a few weeks and being able to telephone them.

She didn't mention the co-operative idea to anyone again and was surprised when Angela brought the subject up as they prepared bowls of vegetables for the evening meal together.

'Nobody has come to buy our gold,' Angela said. 'Some of the men think you have put the evil eye on it.'

Vanessa looked at her horrified.

'The shaman is insisting that you and Ralph attend a village council meeting this evening. He wants to hear what you have to say before deciding what to do.'

'Well done you two,' Nanette said as the twins came running towards her, having been collected by Mathieu from the stage door of the theatre, after performing in their school play. 'You were both brilliant.'

'Wish Mummy could have been here,' Olivia said wistfully.

'I videoed all the bits you and Pierre were in,' Jean-Claude said. 'So Mummy will get to see you. She'll be home in a few weeks.'

'I took some photos on my mobile phone,' Nanette said. 'Here, take a look,' and she handed her phone to Olivia.

As the twins giggled excitedly over the photos, Mathieu asked, 'Would you two like to go for burgers as a special treat?'

'Can we go to that new one down in Fontvielle?' Pierre said.

'Sure, if that's OK with everyone else?' Mathieu said.

Half an hour later as everyone tucked into gigantic

portions of burgers and chips, Jean-Claude's mobile rang. With an apologetic 'Sorry' he excused himself and went outside to answer it.

He didn't say anything when he returned, instead concentrated on helping the twins choose a dessert but Nanette sensed his mood had darkened.

It was late by the time they returned to the apartment and she expected Jean-Claude to say his goodbyes and go straight home. Instead, when Mathieu asked if he was coming up with them he said, 'Yes. I want a word with Nanette.'

Nanette was puzzled, but it wasn't until after the twins were tucked up in bed and Patsy had said goodnight to everyone that he said anything.

'Have you seen Evie recently?'

'Yes,' Nanette said, immediately feeling guilty that she hadn't had time to mention the meeting on board *Pole Position* to Jean-Claude.

'Patsy and I had coffee here with her the other day,' she added. 'I was going to ask if you knew of any PA jobs going. Luc has paid her off and she needs another job. Why do you ask?'

'It was Luc who rang earlier. Don't know the ins and outs of things, but basically he's in real trouble. He got caught up in a business deal that's gone wrong and now he thinks he's being made a scapegoat for others. Did Evie mention any of this when you met?'

Nanette thought about the packet Evie had given her and wished she'd had the chance to talk to JC about it. She shook her head unhappily.

'Is this the Luc I think it is?' Mathieu asked. 'I'd heard his business was in trouble. Give Evie my number – I might be able to help.'

Jean-Claude rounded on his son angrily. 'Oh yes – get her to work with one of your criminal friends. At least it won't be Boris Takyanov now that he's had his application for a resident's visa refused.'

'How do you know that? It's not common knowledge yet,' Mathieu demanded.

'You'd be surprised at just what I do know – including your so called *business activities*, Jean-Claude retorted. 'For instance, I know that you and Zac Ewart had a meeting in Luxembourg recently. I also know you spent six hours in the *gendarmerie* three days ago. I know that Boris—'

'It's you, isn't it?' Mathieu said slowly. 'You're the one having me followed.' He shook his head. 'I can't believe my own father is spying on me.'

'And I can't believe how easily my son has turned from successful businessman into a criminal,' Jean-Claude shouted. '*Oui*, I had you followed because I was worried and wanted to know what was going on so I could help you.'

Both men had forgotten Nanette and she looked from one to the other in dismay as father and son glared at one another.

Mathieu sighed heavily. 'I keep telling you I am not a criminal and don't need you to interfere.'

'Then stop behaving like one and tell me what's going on.'

'I can't. I've been sworn to secrecy. Besides, what you don't know, you can't tell.'

Jean-Claude stared at him. 'I can't believe that you've been stupid enough to get involved with something illegal. These people you're involved with won't hesitate to sacrifice you to save their own skins. And then what happens to the twins?'

Mathieu replied, 'Nanette's here to look after the twins. You, I have no doubt, would also make sure they came to no harm. Vanessa will be home in a few weeks and they will return to England. Meantime, I intend to see this through, whatever you say.'

Jean-Claude shook his head in despair and turned away from his son. Mathieu moved as though to touch him on the arm and say something before changing his mind and walking towards his room instead.

His 'Goodnight' was almost inaudible and the door closed behind him, only to open a second or two later.

'Do me one favour: call off your private detective please.' This time the door closed on his words and stayed shut.

Nanette looking at Jean-Claude's worried face said gently, 'There's nothing you can do, JC.'

'I feel so helpless,' he said, clenching his fists. 'I want to shake him, make him see sense.' He smiled ruefully at her. 'But you are right. This thing has got to run its course whatever the outcome. I can only pray that Mathieu comes out of it unscathed – whatever it may be.'

'Please don't be cross with me, but there is something I should have told you a couple of days ago,' Nanette told him.

Quickly she told Jean-Claude about her visit to *Pole Position* and the package Evie had given her to place in the safe.

'Do you know what was in this package?'

Nanette shook her head and bit her lip before saying quietly, 'I didn't put it in the safe.'

Jean-Claude looked at her surprised. 'What did you do with it?'

'It's in my room,' Nanette said. 'I'll fetch it.'

He turned the package over and over when she handed it to him.

'I suspect it's money,' Nanette said. 'But why would Luc

give money – or anything – to Zac to put in a secret safe?'

Jean-Claude sighed. 'Maybe it's all part of his problems. I'd have said Luc was an honest businessman, but then I'd also have said Mathieu would never get mixed up with anything illegal.' He glanced at her. 'Was there anything in the safe?'

'A gun. Zac would never ever have owned a gun in the past,' she added quietly. 'Shall we open it?' Nanette asked looking first at the package and then at Jean-Claude.

He didn't reply for several minutes and then slowly shook his head.

'Not here. I'll take it with me and put it somewhere safe. I don't feel happy with you having it.' He sighed. 'It's late. Time I went home. I'll be here at about eleven o'clock tomorrow to take Patsy to the airport. Goodnight, *ma chérie.*'

A gentle kiss brushed her cheek and he was gone, leaving Nanette feeling strangely bereft.

There was no sign of Mathieu the next morning before Nanette left to take the twins to school and his bedroom door remained firmly closed. When she returned, Patsy was out on the balcony enjoying her breakfast croissant and coffee.

'I'm going to miss this view,' she said. 'Can't believe in a few hours I'll be back on the farm.' She spread some marmalade on her croissant before adding, 'There's been a lot of activity on *Pole Position* this morning. People coming and going.'

Nanette helping herself to a cup of coffee glanced up. 'What sort of people?'

'Lots of people in suits. Look, there's one of them leaving now.'

The sisters watched as a man carrying a briefcase appeared

in the stern of the yacht with Phil. The two men shook hands and Phil waited as the man left before raising the gangplank and disappearing into the main cabin.

'Hmm,' Patsy said. 'Wonder what that's all about.' She glanced over. 'Bit of a family ding-dong last night?'

Nanette nodded. 'Sorry if it disturbed you. Jean-Claude is getting more and more worried about Mathieu. Unfortunately I don't think there is anything he can do. Have you seen him this morning?'

Patsy shook her head. 'No. Florence said he went out very early.'

Nanette sighed. 'Part of me wishes whatever it is, would all come to a head and hang the consequences – at least we'd all know where we were.'

Patsy stood up. 'Well, I'd better go and finish packing.'

'Need a hand?'

'No thanks. Might need Jean-Claude to carry the suitcase for me though, it's a bit on the heavy side.'

While Patsy finished her packing, Nanette stayed out on the balcony looking down thoughtfully at *Pole Position*. Just what had been happening earlier on the now deserted yacht? Something to do with *Vacances au Soleil* maybe?

Florence, busy cleaning the sitting-room had the radio on softly in the background and Nanette was gently humming along to a favourite song when Jean-Claude arrived.

'How are you today?' she asked, returning his hug and staying in the circle of his arms, concerned at the lines of worry she could see still etched in his face from last night.

Jean-Claude shrugged non-committally. 'I've been better, but I've done as Mathieu asked and called off the private detective.'

'Did he have any final information to give you?'

Jean-Claude glanced towards Mathieu's bedroom door.

'Is he here?'

Nanette shook her head. 'No.'

'Apparently Mathieu has had lots of meetings in recent weeks just over the border in Italy. The detective can't prove it, but he thinks Mathieu was recruiting people to join a business cartel.' Jean-Claude sighed. 'With Boris being refused a permanent visa, I'm afraid that Mathieu will attract more attention from the authorities and move up the list of undesirables. Who knows what will happen then?'

Nanette didn't answer. 'Did you open the package?' she asked instead.

'*Non.*' He shook his head. 'I thought we'd do it together when we get back. Now, is Patsy ready? We should really make a move. I've booked a table for an early lunch in Cannes before we go to the airport.'

Both Nanette and Patsy enjoyed the drive and the lunch Jean-Claude treated them to at one of the restaurants on the Bord de Mer at Cannes. It was 1.30 p.m. as they drove past the roundabout with the preserved prop plane that graced the entrance to Cannes-Mandelieu airport.

'Jean-Claude, thank you for a lovely last day. And for arranging this flight. I still can't believe that I'm going home in a private jet,' Patsy said.

After she'd checked in, Jean-Claude left the two sisters to say their goodbyes.

'You take it easy when you get home,' Nanette said. 'If Helen wants to spoil you – let her!'

'I will,' Patsy promised. She hesitated before continuing, 'Nanette, as much as I would like you to be with me, I will understand if things here make it impossible for you to come back when the bump arrives.'

Nanette hugged her sister. 'Fingers crossed I'll make it. You've got a few weeks to go yet so hopefully things will have sorted themselves out. Vanessa and Ralph might even be back. Now, your flight awaits. Ring me when you get home.'

Nanette left her sister to board the aeroplane and joined Jean-Claude in the car-park where she watched the Lear jet take off with the comforting feel of Jean-Claude's arm around her shoulders.

Settling into the car for the drive back to Monaco, Jean-Claude switched on the car radio as a news bulletin started.

'A failed coup in South America, has led to the arrest of a number of people in Columbia and Brazil.

'And in a series of dawn raids this morning in a joint operation with Interpol, police have arrested a number of men in London and Monaco.'

Jean-Claude and Nanette turned to each other in apprehension, both instantly thinking of Mathieu.

'The arrested men, who include the Russian millionaire, Boris Takyanov, are being held in unnamed police stations. No further details have been given, but it is believed the investigation, code name Sunny Climes, is part of an ongoing inquiry into charges of fraud and tax evasion in Monaco and France.'

Silently Jean-Claude leant forward and turned off the radio before starting the car.

Glancing at Nanette, he said quietly, 'I think we'd better get home as quickly as we can.'

CHAPTER NINE

Nanette was silent, scarcely noticing the kilometres flying past as she sat, immersed in her own thoughts, as Jean-Claude expertly negotiated their way back to Monaco along the auto route.

Jean-Claude had tuned the car radio into the Monte Carlo station frequency hoping to hear some more information about the arrests, but there were no further news bulletins before they arrived back in the Principality.

A worried Florence met them at the apartment door, hysteria in her voice as she said something rapidly to Jean-Claude. The only word Nanette caught and understood was 'Mathieu' and she looked on anxiously as Jean-Claude's expression became grimmer and grimmer before the housekeeper paused for breath.

'She thinks Mathieu's among the men who have been arrested,' Jean-Claude said turning to Nanette. 'I must go and find out; see if there's anything I can do. I'll be back as soon as I can.'

'I need to meet the twins,' Nanette said. 'I'll walk down with you.'

Leaving a clearly worried Jean-Claude at the entrance to the underground garage, Nanette made her way towards the twins' school where Pierre and Olivia were already waiting for her in the playground.

The old port was busy that afternoon with yachts and boats continually making their way in and out of the harbour. Tourists strolled along the embankment taking in the atmosphere and trying to get a glimpse of the celebrities sunbathing on the decks of their large yachts.

Stopping to buy the twins an ice cream at one of the pavement cafés, Nanette watched hundreds of passengers as they disembarked from one of the large ships that spent the summer months cruising the Mediterranean and regularly berthed in the harbour.

Wandering back along the embankment they passed a deserted *Pole Position* – its gangplank raised and the No Entry sign firmly in place. With Zac not due back until shortly before the French Grand Prix the crew would be enjoying having time to themselves.

Briefly, Nanette found herself wishing she didn't have to wait so long to talk to Zac. She desperately needed to discuss her returning memory with him, tell him what she'd decided to do. She wanted to be free to get on with the rest of her life.

Stifling a sigh she shepherded the twins across the road and back to the apartment, hoping to find Jean-Claude and Mathieu there. But Florence was still alone and shook her head when Nanette asked quietly, 'Any news?'

When the phone rang at eight o'clock that night Nanette snatched it up instantly, hoping it was Jean-Claude.

'Hi, Sis,' Patsy's voice said.

'Oh, hi,' Nanette answered, trying to keep the

disappointment out of her voice as she realized it wasn't JC.

'Just ringing to tell you I'm home safely,' Patsy said. 'And that the bump is behaving itself.'

'Great. You take care now for the next few weeks.' Nanette hesitated before adding, 'Patsy, can I ring you for a chat tomorrow? Right now I'm waiting for Jean-Claude to phone.'

'Is everything all right down there?' Patsy asked.

Nanette crossed her fingers before answering. 'Everything is fine. I'll phone you tomorrow and we'll have a chat.'

Once the twins were settled and in bed for the night, Nanette wandered out on to the balcony, unable to concentrate on anything as she waited for news from Jean-Claude.

Down below, Monaco nightlife was buzzing with its usual mid-evening intensity. Yacht crews were welcoming guests on board for dinner, glamorous couples were walking arm in arm along the embankment and the restaurants were full to capacity. The cruise liner Nanette had seen earlier, *Reine Soleil* was slowly manoeuvring its way out of the crowded harbour, beginning its overnight journey to Corsica.

As darkness began to fall, the twinkling reflections of yacht and town lights in the harbour water seemed to Nanette to add a poignant romanticism to the familiar scene. A brief stillness in the night air though filled her with apprehension.

Unexpected tears pricked at the back of her eyes as she suddenly felt very alone and incredibly vulnerable for no real reason that she could fathom. She longed for Jean-Claude to come as she struggled to compose her thoughts.

A matter of minutes later when he did arrive, Nanette surrendered herself totally to the joy of being held in his arms.

'You seem unhappy *ma chérie*?' Jean-Claude said. 'Have you been crying?'

Nanette shook her head. 'Not really. I just felt sad and lonely for some reason. I'm better now you're here.' She stayed happily in the circle of his arms, glancing up at him.

'Now, tell me – is Mathieu in jail?'

'*Non.*' Jean-Claude said. 'But I don't know where he is either. I've contacted everyone I can – even people I wouldn't normally talk to – in the hope that someone would know something, but nothing.' He sighed. 'Maybe tomorrow we'll have some news.' He hesitated. 'I've brought the package with me,' he said quietly. 'I think we open it tonight.'

'Do you think we should?' Nanette said. 'I'm beginning to wish I'd just done as Zac asked and put it in his safe.'

'But, for whatever reason, you didn't,' Jean-Claude said. 'If we open it, it may provide a clue as to what is going on. If not. . . .' He shrugged.

'I think, whatever we find, I ought to put it in the safe before Zac returns,' Nanette said slowly, as she followed Jean-Claude into the sitting-room.

Jean-Claude had placed the package on the table and they both looked at it thoughtfully before he picked it up and examined it.

'Look, if I pull this Sellotape off gently and open it carefully, I can reseal it and Zac need never know we've opened it.'

As he spoke, he gently ran his finger under the seal and carefully eased the package open. Nanette, biting her lips in worry as she watched, felt her mouth forming an astonished 'oh' as she saw the contents slide out of the packaging: a piece of A4 paper with a handwritten list on it and six bottles of shampoo.

Nanette shook her head in disbelief as she looked at Jean-Claude and went to pick up one of the bottles.

'*Non*! Don't touch them,' Jean-Claude said. 'Fingerprints,' he added as Nanette looked at him shocked.

'It's just bottles of shampoo JC,' she protested.

'No, I don't think it's as simple as that,' Jean-Claude said. 'Your prints will be over the outside of the package but you have a legitimate excuse for that. It wouldn't be so easy to explain how your, or my, fingerprints came to be inside on the bottles or the paper. Does Florence have any rubber gloves in the kitchen?'

Nanette nodded. 'I'll fetch them.'

Too small for Jean-Claude's large hands, it was Nanette who put on the gloves.

'Leave the bottles for a moment and put the paper on the table where we can both see it,' Jean-Claude said.

At first glance it appeared to be a jumble of dates, some crossed through, with a single name – either Pepi or Cruz alongside, followed by two initials – RS or MW.

'The dates from April are each roughly a fortnight apart,' Jean-Claude said thoughtfully.

'The exception is the 12 May which is only a week after the preceding one. And that's the only date to have Cruz and MW after it – all the others have Pepi and RS. Is there some sort of pattern here?'

'The crossed-out dates have all gone,' Jean-Claude continued. 'So why haven't the 12 and 19 June been crossed out? We're almost into the last week of June now.'

There was a short silence before Nanette said slowly 'Think about it, JC. It's virtually a Grand Prix timetable. And those two dates coincide with Zac not coming back here after Silverstone, but going straight out to Canada.'

'The next date is three days before the French Grand Prix

next month, when Zac, no doubt, will be back on board *Pole Position*,' Jean-Claude said looking at the list again.

'Now all we've got to do is work out the connection with Pepi, Cruz and what the initials mean,' Nanette replied thoughtfully.

'I can tell you that. Pepi is a crew member on the *Reine Soleil* and Cruz is on the *Mediterranean Wanderer*.'

Jean-Claude and Nanette spun round to see a dishevelled Mathieu regarding them tiredly from the doorway. Carefully Nanette placed the paper on top of the shampoo bottles, forlornly hoping to hide them from Mathieu's view for some reason. But he'd already seen them.

'Where did those come from?' he demanded.

'Never mind those,' Jean-Claude snapped. 'Where the hell have you been?'

Mathieu looked at his father. 'It's a long story that will have to keep until tomorrow.'

He held his hand up to stop Jean-Claude's protestations. 'I promise, you and I will get together tomorrow and I will tell you everything I know.'

'Everything?'

Mathieu nodded. 'Yes. Now, will you please move that paper and let me see those bottles properly.'

Silently Nanette picked up the paper.

'Where did you get these?' Mathieu asked again, as he looked at them.

Nanette hesitated before telling him. 'I was supposed to put them on *Pole Position*.'

Jean-Claude looked at his son. 'These bottles contain something other than shampoo, don't they?'

Mathieu nodded.

'I wondered how they were doing it. I had a good idea how the money laundering was being done but not the actual diamond smuggling.'

'Money laundering? Diamond smuggling?' Nanette said, looking from Jean-Claude to Mathieu. 'Zac?'

'Yes,' Mathieu answered. 'And, I guarantee, if you were to unscrew one of those bottles, more diamonds than you ever thought to see in your life would flow out of those bottles with the shampoo.'

Nanette was returning from taking the twins to school the next morning, when her mobile rang.

'*Chérie*, Luc has asked to meet me this morning. I'll come to the apartment as quickly as I can afterwards. Try not to let Mathieu leave before I get there.'

'I'll do my best,' Nanette promised, not sure how she could detain Mathieu if he decided to leave.

Mathieu was in the small ante-room he was using as a temporary office, working on his computer and listening to an international news bulletin through its speakers when she got back to the apartment.

He glanced up as Nanette opened the door.

'I've brought you a coffee,' Nanette said, handing him a cup. 'Any news about Boris and the others?'

Mathieu shook his head. 'No. But there's some trouble in Formula One,' he said, as the radio bulletin switched to the latest sports news.

'This weekend's US Grand Prix is under threat because of a problem with the tyres. Drivers are threatening to boycott the event over safety fears. Our reporter spoke to current world championship leader, Zac Ewart, earlier.'

Nanette and Mathieu listened as Zac gave his opinion on the problem before saying, 'I'm confident that it will all be sorted within the next forty-eight hours and I fully expect the cars to line up on the grid as usual for this Sunday's race – with me hopefully taking pole position.'

As the news reader went on to the next item, Nanette turned to Mathieu.

'I just don't understand what made Zac get involved with Boris and all this illegal stuff in the first place. He earns so much money from his driving. I know he can't drive for ever, but he was going to build up *Vacances au Soleil* to give him a legitimate business to run when he quits driving. He doesn't need to do illegal stuff.'

Mathieu glanced at her. '*Vacances au Soleil* wasn't going to be a legitimate business. Zac intended it to be a front for more money laundering.'

'But he asked me to work for him. He knows I'd never condone anything illegal,' Nanette protested.

'That's why you'd have been perfect. You'd have handled the day-to-day running of the business honestly, not realizing you were spending money that Zac had come by illicitly.'

'But when he was arrested no-one would have believed that I was innocent,' Nanette said. 'They would have assumed I'd been a part of the conspiracy.'

Mathieu shrugged. 'I guess so.

'As to why he got involved with all this – it's partly excitement, I think,' Mathieu said. 'Something to give him a kick when he loses the adrenalin rush of being able to drive at two hundred miles an hour. Also, it's good, old-fashioned greed.'

'Is that why you got involved – greed?'

Mathieu looked at her steadily. 'Do you really believe that of me, Nanette?'

'Three years ago I wouldn't have believed it of Zac, now,' she shrugged, 'anything seems possible.'

There was a short silence before Mathieu spoke and then he ignored her accusation saying instead, 'I thought my father would be here at the crack of dawn to interrogate me, I wonder where he is. Incidentally, is there something going on between you two?'

Nanette felt the blush spreading across her cheeks and knew denying there was anything between her and Jean-Claude would be silly.

'Thought so,' Mathieu said. 'He's a lucky man.'

'He rang to say he had to go to a meeting and would be later than he intended,' Nanette said. 'He was anxious that you might leave before he gets here.' She glanced at Mathieu. 'He's very worried about what you've got yourself involved in. That you are acting illegally. I hope you can reassure him when he gets here.'

'I certainly intend to explain how and why I got involved, but,' Mathieu hesitated, 'it's not over yet. There are still things I have to do. And whatever he says is not going to stop me doing them.'

Nanette took a sip of her coffee as she regarded Mathieu apprehensively.

'He's more likely to want to help than stop you,' she said. 'To try and prevent you ending up in trouble with the law.'

'Maybe it's time I let him get involved.'

Nanette felt her heart contract at Mathieu's words. The thought of anything happening to Jean-Claude filled her with dread.

'Mathieu—'

'Don't worry. I promise you I won't put him in a direct line of fire.'

Nanette heard the apartment door opening and went to greet Jean-Claude. She needed to feel his arms around her, but wasn't yet ready to display her affection for his father in front of Mathieu.

She returned Jean-Claude's gentle kiss quickly. 'We've been expecting you for ages,' she said.

'Luc needed to talk,' Jean-Claude answered. 'I'll tell you about it later. Where's Mathieu?' he asked anxiously. 'Not disappeared again?'

'Don't worry. I'm in the sitting-room,' Mathieu called out. 'Ready to talk to you.'

'It's about time,' Jean-Claude said, looking at Mathieu expectantly.

'You know I've always kept in touch with Mama's relatives,' Mathieu said. 'Do you remember Uncle Sebastian?'

Jean-Claude nodded. 'Your mama's big brother. Had a restaurant in the centre of Paris for a long time. Didn't he retire a couple of years ago?'

'It was more a case of selling up while he still had something to sell,' Mathieu responded quietly. 'He was being targeted by a protection gang and he simply didn't have the strength to fight Boris Takyanov and his thugs any longer.'

There was a short pause before Mathieu continued 'When Boris turned up in Monaco I knew it wouldn't be too long before he started his criminal activities down here. Anyway, I went to the police to put them in the picture about Takyanov in case the Parisian police hadn't passed on his details. I also offered my help in putting a stop to him.'

Mathieu looked at his father. 'I thought I owed Uncle Sebastian that at least. But the police declined my help – until a few months ago. It was the main reason I couldn't do what Vanessa wanted and look after the twins in the UK,' Mathieu added, turning to Nanette. 'I had to stay here to become a part of the entourage that surrounds Takyanov.'

'The day I arrived and you'd been arrested – was that all part of the plan?' Nanette asked.

Mathieu nodded. 'The police were anxious for me to look like a criminal whom Takyanov would think could be useful to him, so they arrested me on some trumped-up charges. Paying my bail ensured that I had a reason to be grateful to him. His plan, as I suspected, was to muscle in on the local businesses and to run his international operations from here.'

'Luc told me this morning that Boris approached him initially when he first arrived in Monaco, wanting to invest in his business. He was angry when Luc refused,' Jean-Claude said. 'Somehow this year he got wind of the fact that Luc had cash-flow problems and offered to help. Luc says accepting his help was the stupidest decision he has ever made.'

'The parcel Evie delivered to *Pole Position* and Nanette brought here, was the last of several errands that Boris pressured Luc into running for him. He'd decided the only way out of Boris's clutches was to sell up and cease trading – rather like Uncle Sebastian by the sound of it,' Jean-Claude said, looking at Mathieu.

'Did Evie know what she was delivering?' Mathieu asked.

'*Non*. Neither did Luc. When Evie told him Nanette had been there to take the package he was worried that she was involved with Boris. The meeting this morning was to warn me.'

'Do you know how Zac got involved?' Nanette asked. 'He wouldn't have needed a business loan.'

Mathieu shook his head. 'You know Zac and I have been friends for – for ever really. When all this started I had no idea he was caught up in it. I found it very difficult to spy on him. I kept hoping that he'd sort himself out and get free of it, but he's in too deep I'm afraid. I'm sorry,' Mathieu said to Nanette.

She shrugged. 'Zac and I have some personal unfinished business to sort out but he's no longer a part of my life.'

'Why didn't you confide in me before?' Jean-Claude asked quietly.

Mathieu sighed. 'Partly because I didn't want to involve you in case things got nasty, and' – Mathieu hesitated, before adding quietly – 'also because I know how wary you are about Mama's relatives. You'd probably have blamed Uncle Sebastian for getting me involved.'

Jean-Claude shook his head in protest. '*Non.*'

'Anyway, as I told you before, the police urged me to confide in no one,' Mathieu said. 'It was easier that way.'

'Does Takyanov still think you're a fellow criminal?' Jean-Claude asked. 'Even though you haven't been arrested this time?'

'*Oui*. And Zac, too, trusts me – both as his friend and as a fellow conspirator. When he returns for the French Grand Prix I have a feeling he intends to invite me to become more involved in his money-laundering sideline.' Mathieu bit his lip. 'The police have suspected a link between him and Takyanov for a long time but now we have the proof he's involved in the diamond smuggling. Surrendering my friend to the police is going to be one of the hardest things I have ever done.'

'Incidentally, what happened to the shampoo last night?' Jean-Claude asked, looking around as if he expected to see it still on the table. 'I meant to take it and keep it hidden until we decided what to do, but unfortunately your appearance drove it completely out of my mind.'

'I packed it up again,' Nanette answered quietly. 'It's in my room.'

'I think it's too dangerous for you to keep it here,' Jean-Claude said. 'The implications of you being found with it in your possession don't bear thinking about. Perhaps the time has come to hand it over to the authorities?' he continued.

Mathieu shook his head. 'I'd rather not just yet. With Zac out of the country it would only serve to complicate things. Best to keep it hidden until Zac returns and we can confront him with it. If you want me to look after it I will,' he offered.

There was a short silence as Nanette looked from Jean-Claude to Mathieu.

'Personally I think the best place for it is on board *Pole Position*. I really don't know what made me remove it,' she said quietly, shaking her head. 'At least if it's in the safe when Zac gets back, he doesn't need to know that I didn't do as he asked.'

She took a deep breath and cut short both Jean-Claude and Mathieu's protestations.

'As I'm the one who took it and the only one who knows where the safe is, as well as the combination to open it, the responsibility to return it is mine.'

Vanessa wiped her sleeve across her face in the forlorn hope of mopping up some of the perspiration that was making her face itch. Her hair under her hat was wet and sweat was beginning to drip down her neck.

It was three hours now since they'd said goodbye to the villagers and Luigi their guide had led them into the jungle to begin their long trek back to civilization.

The last thirty-six hours had been hard. Not only was their stay in the village coming to an end with Ralph unable to complete his film the way he wanted, it now seemed the friendships they'd forged with the villagers were about to be torn apart by some superstition.

Summoned to the village council, they'd apprehensively followed Angela to the main hut on the evening of what should have been their last night in the village.

As far as Vanessa could see every villager from the smallest newborn baby to the oldest native, were waiting for them, grim-faced. The hunters had returned early from a food foraging expedition and were now grouped around the head shaman, still clutching their spears, staring intently at Vanessa and Ralph.

Vanessa shivered. Did they really believe she and Ralph had put the 'evil eye' on their gold? Memories of a terrifying visit as a young girl to a museum exhibition of cannibalism and shrunken heads suddenly sprang unbidden into her mind. Those practices might have been outlawed but what if other macabre rituals had taken their place?

Swallowing hard to stop the bile in her throat rising, Vanessa looked fearfully at the natives she'd treated as friends for several weeks.

There was a stranger, his skin glistening with sweat, his spears and machete strapped in place on his back, talking and gesturing with the head shaman. Vanessa glanced at him curiously.

'He's one of the native runners who keep all the villages in touch. Apparently he's brought some urgent news,' Ralph told her, after a quick consultation with Angela.

Luigi, who with Nick the cameraman, was acting as interpreter, moved forward and listened intently to what the man was saying. Vanessa clutched at Ralph's hand nervously as silence descended in the hut and the head shaman turned and beckoned them forward.

'We have news that Maksim, the outsider, has been detained. His word has been broken. It is not you who have cast the evil eye.' He paused. 'We are free to trade with you.'

Vanessa felt her whole body shudder in relief. But then she looked at Nick and Luigi aghast. The villagers had clearly misunderstood what she was offering to do.

'Nick, Luigi, before this goes any further, you must make them understand the Fruits of the Forest co-operative would be their responsibility. I'm not buying their produce, only helping them to get organized to sell it.'

Once she was convinced that the villagers, and the head shaman in particular, understood exactly what she was proposing, Vanessa felt the tension leave her body and she quickly began to outline again all the things the villagers would need to do to get the co-operative up and running.

'I just wish we weren't leaving tomorrow,' she said. 'There's so much to explain and put into action.'

'We can stay one more day if you like,' Ralph offered. 'No longer though, Nick and Harry have work commitments to get back for.'

Vanessa and Ralph worked into the small hours trying to sort out a basic businesslike plan of campaign to get the co-operative off the ground. In the morning they held their own village council meeting to tell the head shaman and the villagers the things they needed to do.

The extra day had been a busy one with so many things to organize, not least packing up some samples of the native medicines, including several pots of the Sangre de Grado ointment that had helped Ralph's injuries to heal so well.

'If only we'd thought of this when we first arrived,' Vanessa said. 'I could have done so much more before having to leave them to get on with it.' She sighed and looked at Ralph. 'There is one thing that still worries me though. What happens if this Maksim comes back and tries to muscle in on the co-operative? Angela did say the men knew there were dangers in upsetting him.'

'Don't worry. Once we get back to civilization we can alert the authorities to what we are doing. We need to organise sponsors and then we can appoint an overseer to come out here to supervise things in your absence. Make sure there are no disruptions. You'll be amazed at the progress on your next visit, you'll see,' Ralph said confidently.

Hugging Angela goodbye the following morning, Vanessa was surprised to find herself fighting back the tears. 'I'll miss you,' she said. 'But I will be back.'

'Goodbye, Pacchumama. May the spirits be with you on your journey,' Angela said, returning the hug.

Now, as she tiredly followed Luigi and the porters along the muddy track, Vanessa's mind was still racing, trying to sort out the logistics of the co-operative and wondering who she'd be able to find willing to sponsor Fruits of the Forest for at least its first year in business.

Darkness had descended as they reached the native camp where they were to spend their last night in the jungle proper.

Tiredly Vanessa stumbled into their sleeping hut.

Tomorrow they would travel by small canoe up the feeder river to the Amazon itself and then a larger boat would take them to the town of Manaus. Their journey home had begun.

'Right you two. Dry yourselves off, get dressed and go to the games room while I have a quick swim. Papa Jean-Claude will be here soon and then we'll have some supper before we go home.'

Nanette had taken the twins up to the villa after school for their usual afternoon swim. To her disappointment there had been no sign of Jean-Claude. His housekeeper had merely told her, '*Monsieur* had to go out for a couple of hours.'

Lazily floating on her back after completing a couple of energetic laps, Nanette found herself thinking about Mathieu's revelations and the package currently concealed under her bed.

Somehow she had to find the right moment to go inconspicuously to *Pole Position* and put it in the safe.

She heard the twins calling out '*Bonjour, Papa Jean-Claude,*' and quickly swam to the steps and got out of the pool. Before she could pick up her towel Jean-Claude appeared and took her in his arms.

'I'll make you all wet,' Nanette protested weakly, before she surrendered herself to his embrace.

Several minutes passed before Nanette sighed and drew away. 'I think you'd better let me get dressed before the twins come demanding to be fed,' she said regretfully, giving Jean-Claude one last lingering kiss.

It was early evening when Nanette left to take the twins back to the apartment. Olivia and Pierre had already kissed their grandfather goodbye and were waiting for Nanette out on the terrace when Jean-Claude said to Nanette, 'I've been thinking about the package. If you are determined to replace it – and I agree that would probably be for the best – I will come with you. I think tomorrow morning after the twins go to school *n'est pas*? I will wait on the quay, while you go on board.'

Nanette hesitated before saying, 'Perhaps Mathieu ought to come with me instead. The police have involved him officially, whereas you. . . .' Her voice trailed off.

'*Non*. I'm coming with you.'

Nanette smiled, before kissing him gently.

'OK. Thanks. Now, I'm going home to get the twins to bed and I think I might have an early night myself. I'll see you in the morning.'

But when Nanette did go to bed, soon after the twins, she tossed and turned restlessly. She had been convinced she was so tired she would have no problems sleeping but the hot midsummer night air was stifling. Even the ceiling fan silently whirring away above her head was failing to keep her cool.

It wasn't just the heat keeping her awake. Her mind was tossing and turning, too. All day Mathieu's words 'it isn't over yet' had been playing on her mind.

She knew Boris was still in jail having been refused bail and the latest rumour flying around Monaco was that Interpol had arrested his son. More arrests were expected to be made soon. Was that going to include Zac Ewart?

Mathieu had spent most of the day in the apartment after warning them that things were likely to come to a head soon and he wanted to keep a low profile for a few days.

Unable to sleep and sighing in frustration, Nanette got out of bed. Pulling on her dressing-gown she went through the silent apartment to the kitchen to fetch a glass of water. A dim light was shining under the threshold of Mathieu's door, everywhere else was in darkness.

Returning to her room she opened the curtains and pushed the balcony door open. The breeze from the harbour ruffled her hair but was too hot to bring any relief from the heat.

Glancing down at the harbour Nanette was struck by a sudden idea as she looked at *Pole Position* gently moving on its mooring.

The lights were on in the main saloon of the yacht – that had to mean only one thing: the crew, or at least Phil, the skipper, was still up.

Ten minutes – fifteen at the most – was all it would take to go down, put the package in the safe and return to the apartment. The quay was relatively empty of people, just a few couples taking a romantic night-time stroll.

With luck, nobody would even notice her. She'd be able to tell JC in the morning he needn't worry about accompanying her to the yacht. The package was back where it should be. She could no longer be linked to the contents.

Quickly putting on a pair of jeans and a dark top, she slipped her feet into her docksiders, before pulling the box from under the bed and taking out the *Vacances au Soleil* papers as well as the package. If the luxury holiday business was a front for money laundering as Mathieu had said, those papers, too, would be better back on board.

Picking up her keys, she quietly left the apartment. Once on the quay alongside *Pole Position*, Nanette was surprised to find that although the 'No Entry' sign was in place, the gangplank to the yacht was lowered so she simply walked on board. The door to the main cabin was closed and, as she opened it, Phil glanced up from the table where he was working on some papers.

'Hi. I just need to put these in Zac's safe,' Nanette said confidently, as she walked past him towards the master bedroom, willing him not to stop her.

Phil looked as though he was about to say something and then simply shrugged his shoulders and returned to his paperwork.

Nanette didn't bother to throw the light switch in the bedroom – there was enough light from the passageway for her to see her way across. In the bathroom, she pushed the door to as she switched on the mirror lights before kneeling down and moving the towels and lifting the under sink shelf out.

Once again she concentrated on remembering the combination number and breathed a sigh of relief as she pulled the safe door open. She was doing what she should have done originally – putting the package in the safe.

Another minute and she'd be on her way back to the apartment. Her actions froze as her gaze took in the empty shelf where the gun had been: there was only one person in the world who could have removed it.

The door behind her creaked. Slowly she raised her head. A cold shiver ran through her as she recognized the body of the man reflected in the illuminated bathroom mirror.

Nanette watched, rigid with fear, as Zac Ewart casually flipped off the safety catch before levelling the gun at her and asking, 'Why, oh why, did you have to meddle, Nanette?'

CHAPTER TEN

Night-time sounds of the crew moving about up on deck punctuated the silence as Zac regarded Nanette intently, the gun steady in his hand.

'Do you intend using that, or shall I put it back in the safe too?' Nanette asked quietly.

Zac looked at the gun as if he'd forgotten he was holding it, and shrugged. 'Might as well.'

As he leant forward and handed her the gun he said, 'Don't worry, it's not loaded.'

Wordlessly Nanette took the gun from him and put it in the safe.

'Why didn't you put the package in the safe the other day?'

Nanette swallowed hard. 'Couldn't remember the combination,' she said finally.

'Oh, and now you can. Came to you in a flash, did it? Incidentally, I'll have the *Vacances au Soleil* papers if that's what's in the envelope. They don't need to go in the safe.'

Silently Nanette handed the envelope up to him.

'You lied to me, didn't you, Zac, when you told me there was nothing illegal about the package?'

Zac shrugged. 'Did you open it?'

Nanette flushed but didn't answer.

Zac's eyes narrowed.

'You did. I trust you didn't go as far as using any of the contents? Or, indeed, showing them to anyone else?'

'Why would I show bottles of shampoo to anyone?' Nanette said, as innocently as she could. Nothing would induce her to tell Zac that Jean-Claude had been with her when she opened the parcel – or that Mathieu had also seen the contents and told her what they contained.

'Good. Well, go on – put it in the safe.'

He watched as she carefully did as she was told and closed the door.

'Don't forget to leave everything tidy, will you?' he said, looking at the shelf and the towels on the floor, before turning on his heels and leaving Nanette alone in the bathroom.

Nanette steadied herself against the cupboard as the yacht rocked unexpectedly on her mooring. Shakily, she started to replace the shelf before reaching for the towels. Only a few more minutes and she'd be on her way home.

Another unexpected movement of the yacht and Nanette frowned. Something big must have come into the harbour to cause such a rocking wake. It was almost as if *Pole Position* was underway. Nanette felt her body freeze at the thought.

Leaving the towels on the floor and slamming the bathroom door behind her she ran to the nearest porthole in the master bedroom.

Monaco town lights were fading into indistinguishable specks along the shoreline. The walls that guarded the entrance of the harbour were disappearing from view as the yacht made for the open sea.

'Nice evening for a trip round the bay, don't you think?'

Nanette spun round to see Zac watching her lazily from the large king-sized bed.

'Turn the yacht around and let me off,' Nanette demanded.

Zac shook his head. 'Sorry, I can't do that. We have to talk.'

Nanette glared at him. 'If I'm not there to take the twins to school tomorrow morning, Mathieu will be worried.'

Zac shrugged. 'I spoke to him on the satellite phone a few minutes ago. I told him you were spending the night with me.'

Nanette flushed angrily at the implication behind his words.

'If you don't turn around immediately, the first thing I shall do when I get back is go to the authorities and have you charged with kidnapping,' Nanette threatened.

'They'd just think you were a spurned lover – after all you were happy enough to come aboard before. Besides, you did come aboard of your own free will. Phil will attest to that.'

Disconsolate and fighting back tears Nanette stared at him. It seemed a long time ago that she had thought she loved this man.

'How long do you intend to keep me on board?'

Before Zac could answer there was a discreet knock on the cabin door.

'The saloon is ready sir,' the head stewardess said.

Zac turned to Nanette. 'You told me recently we needed a serious talk so, shall we be civilized and do it over a meal?'

'Answer my question. How long?'

Zac sighed before saying slowly, 'As long as necessary. Now, shall we eat? What with the flight back and the time difference I haven't eaten for hours.'

'I'm not hungry,' Nanette said.

'Suit yourself. You can talk to me while I eat.'

Two places were laid on the mahogany dining-table – crystal glasses, silver cutlery and candles in gold candelabra gave a gentle glow to the cabin. Champagne nestled in a silver ice bucket, while a CD of guitar music was playing softly in the background.

'Just like the old days when we were together,' Zac said.

'Hardly,' Nanette snapped.

Zac poured a glass of champagne and offered it to her. When Nanette shook her head and turned away he raised the glass in a mock salute before taking a long drink and then topping up the glass.

'What are you doing here anyway?' Nanette asked. 'Why aren't you still in America?'

'Only five drivers were going to trust their tyres enough to line up on the grid – as none of them is anywhere near me in the championship I decided I could boycott the race too without it affecting my title chances,' he answered. 'So, as I've got some urgent business to sort out here, I caught the first available flight back.'

He helped himself to a portion of smoked salmon.

'Vanessa is due back soon, isn't she? Thought anymore about working with me on *Vacances au Soleil*? We could be a good team again. I'll even make you a director if you want. I'm hoping Mathieu is going to join the company too in the near future.'

Nanette, about to protest that Mathieu definitely wouldn't be joining him and that she knew *Vacances au Soleil* was a front for a money laundering operation, stopped. Zac didn't yet know the part Mathieu was about to play in his downfall.

'The answer is still no, Zac. I won't work for you again.' She paused. 'Besides, I'm not entirely convinced you're not lying to me when you say it's a legal business.'

Zac eyed her over the top of his champagne flute.

'You lied to me – to everyone – three years ago, about the accident, didn't you, Zac?' she said, watching his face for a reaction to her words.

'I wasn't driving that night, was I, Zac? What I don't understand is why you lied? Why you ruined my life?'

In the silence that followed her words, Zac impassively forked some food into his mouth.

Nanette felt her temper rising. He could he be so indifferent to what she was saying, to her feelings? He didn't care. Had he ever really cared?

'I remember driving to the restaurant,' Nanette continued softly. 'You offered to drive back so I could enjoy the wine with my meal. All evening, apart from a single glass of champagne to toast my birthday, you drank water.'

Nanette took a deep breath.

'I remember you getting into the driver's seat when we left the restaurant. So, why after the accident, did you deliberately make it look as though I'd been driving? You knew the wine and the champagne I'd drunk during the evening would have put me way over the limit, whereas you were sober.' Nanette held her breath waiting for his reaction.

Zac sighed before finally looking her in the eye.

'Couldn't you just see the headlines in the *Nice Matin* – "Formula 1 Ace charged with dangerous driving"? So, when the *pompiers* arrived and assumed you were the driver as it was your car, I decided not to enlighten them.'

'It was very convenient for you then, that I lost my memory

for so long, wasn't it? Couldn't speak up and set the story straight.'

Zac didn't reply.

'Is that why you didn't come near me again? Why you had me airlifted back to the UK? You were afraid that I would suddenly broadcast to the world that I wasn't actually driving when the car aquaplaned. It was a famous racing driver who had taken the coward's way out!'

'I did pull you out of the wreckage before it burst into flames. I deserve some credit for that, don't I?' Zac asked quietly.

Nanette glared at him. 'What you did afterward was despicable, Zac.'

'The media would have crucified me, Nanette. I was at a critical point of my career – just changing teams – I didn't need the wrong sort of publicity. You on the other hand' – he shrugged before giving her a sardonic smile – 'who was going to really care whether you lost your licence? You were just my girlfriend, no one special in the eyes of the world.'

As he stared her down, defying her to argue with him, Nanette knew that any lingering love she had once felt for Zac Ewart had just been bludgeoned to death by his callous words.

'Tomorrow I am going to start clearing my name,' she said defiantly.

'Why bother after all this time? Besides, who are people going to believe: a world-famous racing driver or a one-time office girl?' He hesitated before adding quietly, 'I did try once, Nanette, to set the record straight, but by then the police had done their paperwork and it was too late.'

'If you had any decency left you'd come with me and make

them acknowledge the truth.'

Nanette gazed reflectively at Zac. Life on the race track was a serious business, not to be taken lightly, but away from the circuit Zac had always had this cavalier attitude to life. It had been one of the things she'd found difficult to accept about him. Jean-Claude, she knew, would never have deserted her in her hour of need. That Jean-Claude would always be there for her, she didn't doubt for a single second.

'Nanette, what are you thinking? You're miles away. I remember you getting that dreamy look when we were together. Are you thinking about us?'

Nanette shook her head. 'Oh no, Zac. I'm not taking a trip down memory lane with you. I'm thinking about my future and you are staying firmly in the past.'

'Have you met someone else?'

'Yes,' Nanette said simply. 'Someone very special. Someone who truly loves me.'

Nanette didn't understand the pained look that crossed Zac's face, but she did realize that he clearly hadn't been expecting that answer from her.

There was a short silence, before he said slowly, 'I hope things work out for you.'

He continued, 'Things in my life have changed, too, in the last three years. There are different things at stake.'

'Things like your business deals with that criminal Boris Takyanov? You know, Zac,' Nanette said thoughtfully, 'I never had you down as a common criminal. How did that happen?'

Zac was silent for several seconds before saying, 'I stupidly got myself involved in something I shouldn't have. The next thing I knew Takyanov made me an offer I couldn't refuse –

didn't dare refuse,' he added quietly. 'And now I'm in too deep for him to let me go.'

'He's blackmailing you? Oh Zac, what a mess,' Nanette said sadly. 'Well, I can't see him doing much in the way of business from Monaco jail,' Nanette said.

Zac spun round from the table where he was helping himself to yet more champagne. 'Takyanov's been arrested?'

'Yes. Hadn't you heard? Along with several of his so-called business associates.'

Zac pushed past her and opened the cabin door.

'Phil, turn around and take us back to harbour *now*,' he shouted.

Nanette heard the skipper's answering 'Will do', felt *Pole Position* change course and breathed a sigh of relief. This nightmare would soon be over.

Unexpectedly he grabbed her hand. 'I need some air. Come on, let's go out on deck and watch the lights.'

As Zac pulled her towards the yacht's bow, Nanette was struck by an irrational fear. Could he possibly be planning to push her overboard and claim it was an accident?

The city of Manaus was a huge shock to Vanessa. Ralph had told her it was one of the most isolated metropolitan areas in the world but she was ill prepared for its vastness and the noise it generated.

As their boat drew alongside the floating dock she stood up and looked around. Seven hours ago the boat had been moored in a quiet tributary with jungle animal sounds providing the background noise and happy smiling natives helping them load the boat for the journey up-river.

Here, moored on the banks of the Amazon River itself, it

was the raucous sounds of a modern industrial jungle that surrounded them as they stepped off the boat. It was hard to believe that this busy inland port was in the heart of the rain forest.

Vanessa gazed fascinated at the double-decked ferries and houseboats that were everywhere, crammed along the shoreline in front of ramshackle buildings on the water's edge. Dozens of large cargo ships were tied up unloading goods, others were taking on board sacks of coffee beans, rubber, and nuts. All, it seemed to Vanessa, in vast quantities. She glanced at her husband.

'Do you think anyone is going to be interested in shipping the small quantities of produce Fruits of the Forest is going to have in the beginning?'

'Of course,' Ralph said confidently. 'We'll look for a small commercial shipper who is keen to expand and grow with the co-operative. No point in even approaching the big international boys in the beginning. We'll ask around tomorrow. Right now, let's get to the hotel.'

The hotel, a tall modern building ten minutes from the city centre, was blessedly cool after the humidity outside.

Once they were registered, Ralph asked the receptionist to book a phone call to Monaco for them, and they went straight to their room.

When the phone on the bedside table rang, Vanessa snatched it up only to be told the number wasn't answering and the receptionist would try again later.

'Perhaps by then we'll have a definite UK arrival date,' Ralph said trying to ease her disappointment. 'Nick and Harry are going out to the airport later to try and book flights.'

'Do you feel up to doing some exploring?' Ralph continued. 'Might as well see the sights.'

'Can we leave the touristy bit until tomorrow? What I really want to do is have a shower, something to eat and go to bed. I'm exhausted,' Vanessa said.

'Sure. In that case I'll go out to the airport with the boys. Do you want me to order you something from room service, or will you go down to the dining-room?'

'A sandwich from room service would be fine.'

After her shower Vanessa curled up on the double bed to eat her supper revelling in the air-conditioned coolness of the room. She'd forgotten during the last few months in the jungle what it was like to be comfortable and not continually damp with perspiration.

Ralph returned with frustrating news. 'I'm sorry, Vanessa, I know you're desperate to get home to the twins, but there are no direct flights available. We've got to go via the States. And even then we can't fly for forty-eight hours.'

Vanessa hid her disappointment. 'Can't be helped. Hopefully I'll get to speak to them tomorrow.' She glanced at Ralph, hot and sticky from his foray to the airport.

'Why don't you have a shower and then come to bed? It's far more comfy than the hammocks we've been using recently.'

The next morning they were up early intent on getting down to the docks to look for a shipper exporter willing to discuss handling the Fruits of the Forest produce. Vanessa also wanted to explore the Mercado Adolpho Lisboa, the city's oldest market place.

Their search around the docks for a shipping company proved fruitless. Nobody even had the time to speak to them, let alone discuss exporting Fruits of the Forest produce.

'Let's give up,' Vanessa said. 'I've a feeling it's going to be easier to organize it through a third party from the UK.'

Before returning to the hotel they wandered through the vast ancient market thronging with locals buying their produce from the traditional stalls. The outside streets were packed with more stalls and souvenir sellers. Vanessa was delighted to find a stall selling the locally made woven bags and ponchos.

'Nanette will adore one of the bags,' she said. 'And I'll get a couple of ponchos for the twins.'

Back in their hotel room Vanessa booked a call to Monaco. Standing, receiver in hand, she listened to the ringing tone before shaking her head at Ralph.

'Still no reply. I don't understand it. Oh ... hello Jean-Claude? Where is everyone? I was just about to hang up.'

Vanessa was silent as she listened to Jean-Claude for several minutes.

'OK. Will you tell Nanette I'll ring her tomorrow then with our plans? Yes, we've had a great time. Hope to see you soon. Goodbye.' Vanessa slowly replaced the receiver before turning to look at Ralph.

'That was weird. Neither Mathieu nor Nanette were in the apartment. Jean-Claude wouldn't tell me where they were although he assured me the twins are fine. I'm worried now. Something is going on back there.'

Dawn was breaking over a sleeping Monaco as *Pole Position* sailed towards the harbour entrance. Nanette, standing in the cockpit, felt an overwhelming sense of relief sweep through her body. Another half-hour and she would be back on dry land.

A tense Zac had insisted they spent the entire return journey up on deck and now Nanette watched the shore lights getting closer with unconcealed pleasure.

As Phil carefully positioned the yacht to motor slowly into her allocated berth and the crew tied the large navy fenders in place, Zac turned to her.

'I guess you and I are all washed up now. No chance of even remaining friends?'

'We were all washed up, as you put it, when you decided to lie about the accident,' Nanette said, watching Phil press the button to lower the gangplank. 'I can never forgive you for that.'

Zac suddenly turned her to face him, gripping both her arms tightly.

'Stop it, Zac, you're hurting me.'

The pressure increased on her arms as Zac ignored her words and squeezed harder. Nanette closed her eyes, willing him to stop inflicting pain, and waiting for him to release her.

'You think this hurts? Be warned, Nanette – it's nothing to what could happen. Other people don't have my scruples – or share a past with you. Do one last thing for me: walk away from whatever you think is going on.'

The grip on her arms lessened and Nanette opened her eyes to see Zac staring at her intently.

'Goodbye, Zac,' she said. Trembling, she moved away from him towards the gangplank desperate to put as much space between her and Zac Ewart as possible.

Blinded by the tears that had started to run down her cheeks, she didn't see Jean-Claude standing on the quay with Mathieu until it was too late and she'd run into him.

'*Doucement, ma chérie,*' he said, gently enveloping her in his arms. *'Doucement.* I'm here now to take care of you.'

The gentle kiss he placed on her forehead wasn't enough for Nanette. She turned and looked at him before hesitantly kissing him deliberately on the lips. As she surrendered herself to Jean-Claude's passionate embrace, she was conscious of a statue-like Zac watching them with an unfathomable look on his face.

It was the swish of the curtains that woke Nanette and she blinked as sunlight flooded the bedroom. Jean-Claude had entered the room quietly and placed a tray of coffee and croissants on the bedside table before crossing to the window to open the curtains.

Nanette smiled sleepily to herself as she watched him. He'd been insistent she go to bed after he'd brought her back to the apartment early that morning.

'I'll take the twins to school if Mathieu hasn't returned. You get some sleep. Afterwards you can explain exactly why you went alone to the yacht,' he'd said.

Nanette had done as she was told and gone to bed. To her surprise within minutes she'd fallen into a deep dreamless sleep.

'What's the time?' she asked, sitting up as Jean-Claude placed the tray on her lap.

'One o'clock. How do you feel?'

'Fine.'

'Are you ready to tell me why you went alone to *Pole Position*?'

Nanette, about to answer flippantly 'It seemed a good idea at the time', looked at his concerned expression and said quietly, 'I'm sorry, Jean-Claude.'

She stretched out a hand to gently touch his face.

'At least he didn't push me overboard as I thought he might do at one stage,' she said quietly.

Jean-Claude looked at her horrified. '*Mon Dieu*. I would kill him if he hurt you.'

'Any hurt Zac inflicted on me is now in the past. I have no intention of going anywhere near him in the future,' Nanette said, tiredly. 'I'll tell you all about last night but first I must get up. Give me ten minutes to shower and dress.'

'I'll wait for you in the sitting-room,' Jean-Claude said, kissing her gently on the cheek as he took the tray. 'Take your time.'

Half an hour later, Nanette joined him on the balcony where he was reading a newspaper.

'The charges against Takyanov are getting longer by the day,' he said folding the newspaper. 'And more people are being drawn into the net.'

'Is Mathieu around?' Nanette asked.

'No,' Jean-Claude shook his head. 'No idea where he's gone. Vanessa phoned while you were sleeping. She and Ralph arrive back in the UK next week. She wants you to take the twins over. She said something about her and Ralph taking them on holiday. Anyway, she's going to phone you this evening to discuss it.'

Nanette looked at Jean-Claude in dismay. She'd forgotten Vanessa's return would signal the end of her stay in Monaco. 'Next week?'

Jean-Claude caught hold of her hands. 'You leave the twins with Vanessa and come back to me, yes? You will have some holiday due?'

'Patsy's baby is due soon. If I'm in England I'll have to be there for that. Maybe afterwards? But where would I stay? Mathieu won't want me in the apartment without the twins.'

'At the villa, no question. My housekeeper will prepare the guest suite, and look after us.' Jean-Claude took her in his arms. 'It will be wonderful, *chérie*. Just you and me. Getting to know each other properly. We'll swim, relax, go to Italy.'

Nanette smiled at him. 'Sounds wonderful. Maybe by the time I get back all this business with Mathieu and Takyanov will be resolved. Has Mathieu accepted your offer of help?'

Jean-Claude gave a shrug. 'Apparently there is not a lot I can do – simply wait in the shadows and be ready to make a move when he asks – *if* he asks.'

'Maybe that's for the best,' Nanette said. 'He's always said you must trust him; he knows what he's doing.'

'Which is more than you did last night,' Jean-Claude said. 'I couldn't believe it when Mathieu rang to say that Zac had told him you were spending the night with him.'

'I couldn't sleep and it seemed like an ideal opportunity to get rid of the package,' Nanette said. 'If I'd known Zac was on board I certainly wouldn't have gone.'

Hesitantly she began to tell Jean-Claude about the previous night's events. She glossed over her terror when she realized they had put to sea. Jean-Claude she knew would be furiously protective on her behalf.

'At least Zac has finally acknowledged the truth about the accident,' she said. 'He was driving the night of the accident. He lied to the *pompiers* and the *gendarmes*. My loss of memory for so long was very convenient for him.' Nanette took a deep breath.

'I told him I was going to the authorities to clear my name. Although he reckons I'd be wasting my time because people wouldn't believe me.' She bit her lip. 'Until last night I hadn't realized how deep the scars were – how much the past was damaging my present. But I've decided not to try and clear my name. I will walk away from it. I need to relegate it to the past and forget it. Move on with my life.'

Lovingly Jean-Claude took her in his arms.

'I can never forgive him for what he did, but it's not worth dragging it all up again,' Nanette said, as he bent his head to kiss her. 'You know the truth and that's all that really matters to me now.'

As the taxi pulled into the farmyard, the driver, a local man who knew Patsy and Nanette, nodded in the direction of a battered red Mini parked by the hay barn.

'Reckon you'm an aunty,' he said sagely. 'That's Dr Owen's car.'

'Reckon you could be right,' Nanette said, fishing in her bag for the fare.

Helen came bustling out of the kitchen. 'It's a boy,' she said, seeing Nanette. 'I've got a grandson, imagine!'

'Can I go up and see them?' Nanette asked.

'Doctor's with Patsy at the moment. Come into the kitchen and I'll make some tea. You can take a cup up to Patsy.'

It was half an hour before Nanette opened the bedroom door and peered round.

'Hi, Mum! Congratulations.'

Patsy, cradling her new son, smiled at her sleepily. 'Hi, Aunty. Didn't you time your arrival well? Meet your nephew – all seven pounds two ounces of him.' Patsy held out the tiny bundle and Nanette tentatively took the precious cargo into her arms.

Unexpectedly she found herself wondering, was this the closest she was going to get to having a baby of her own?

'He's gorgeous. So much hair,' Nanette said. 'Any names yet?'

Patsy shook her head. 'Helen is all for Hew Trefor.' She laughed at Nanette's expression. 'Apparently they're very old family names – Bryan's middle name is Hew. But I fancy Dylan Robert.'

'The new granny is beside herself with joy,' Nanette said. 'I don't suppose she'll care what you call him so long as she's allowed to spoil him. Dylan's a nice name.' Nanette smiled down at the baby boy.

'Bryan and I are hoping you will be a godmother,' Patsy said.

'I'd love to.'

'Good. Any ideas who you'd like to see in the godfather role?' Patsy asked innocently.

Nanette laughed and shook her head before asking, 'Shall I put Dylan in his cradle?'

'Please. How long can you stay?' Patsy asked, watching as Nanette gently placed a cover over the sleeping baby.

'A few days. Vanessa and Ralph have taken the twins to Cornwall and I'm officially on holiday for the next fortnight.'

'Why can't you stay longer then?'

'I've promised to return to Monaco and spend the time with Jean-Claude,' Nanette said, blushing.

Patsy looked at her sister speculatively. 'Are you going to tell me any more?'

Nanette shook her head. 'Not right now. I'm sure you need your rest. I promise we'll talk later when you're up and about. I could do with some sisterly advice.'

Two days later, sitting companionably under the shade of the horse chestnut tree that dominated the side garden, sipping cold lemonade with Dylan asleep in his pram beside them, Nanette talked to Patsy about her worries for the future.

'I've got to decide what I want to do. Vanessas's come back fired up with enthusiasm for starting a Fruits of the Forest co-operative in Brazil. The twins are growing up and don't need a nanny twenty-four hours a day now so she's offering me the job of helping her organize it – getting sponsorship, outlets, all the legal bits and pieces, you know the sort of thing.'

'Sounds like something you'd enjoy,' Patsy said. 'I'd guess there would be a few trips to Brazil too.'

'The thing is, the whole business would be based in the UK and. . . .' Nanette sighed.

'Jean-Claude is in Monaco,' Patsy finished the sentence for her. 'Is it serious between you two?'

'On Jean-Claude's part for several weeks,' Nanette admitted. 'And now that my memory's returned and the whole Zac Ewart business has been finished with, I feel free to return his love. You don't think he's too old for me?' she asked her sister anxiously.

Before Patsy could answer, Dylan stirred in his pram and Nanette got up to check on her nephew. Picking him up and cradling him in her arms she sat back down in the shade.

'From what I've seen of the two of you, you're perfect together. He adores you and no, of course he's not too old,' Patsy said. 'But it might be wise to check with him how he feels about babies, if you're thinking of having a family with him. He might feel, been there, done that and just want you to himself.'

*

Nanette picked up a magazine and a paper from the newsagent in the departure lounge Monday afternoon and settled down to wait for her flight back to Nice.

She'd enjoyed her few days with Patsy and baby Dylan but had missed Jean-Claude desperately. She smiled happily to herself – a few more hours and they would be together with no responsibilities to worry about, just time to enjoy each other's company.

The newspaper was full of Zac's performance in the French Grand Prix the previous day. He'd driven a faultless race and won convincingly, according to the reporter. His nearest rival for the championship had only managed ninth place thus increasing Zac's lead substantially.

Nanette stared dispassionately at the photograph of Zac standing jubilantly on the podium, before turning to the women's pages. Zac Ewart was no longer a part of her life. She wouldn't waste her time reading about him.

Three hours later she stretched her legs as the captain's voice crackled through the intercom of the 737.

'Welcome to the French Riviera. The temperature at Nice and along the Côte d'Azure is 33 degrees and the forecast is good for the next few days.

Collecting her suitcase from the carousel, Nanette looked through the glass windows towards the Arrivals Hall. As he'd promised, Jean-Claude was there waiting for her. She smiled happily and waved. Exiting the door from the final Customs Checkpoint she walked towards him looking forward to his welcoming kiss.

Surrendering herself to his arms, oblivious to the milling

crowds, she sensed a tension in his body.

'Is something wrong? Has something happened to Mathieu?'

'*Non*, it's not Mathieu. Let's have a coffee before we drive home,' Jean-Claude said, taking her suitcase and leading her to the escalator to go to the fourth floor. Seated at a window table of La Badiane lounge with its view out over the runway, Jean-Claude ordered two coffees.

Taking both of Nanette's hands in his he said grimly, 'Zac drove home from the French Grand Prix via his friends the Oliviers. They have a farm up in the hills – do you remember them?'

Nanette nodded. 'We used to visit them a lot.'

'He left early this morning and got involved in an incident on one of the isolated mountain roads.'

'What sort of incident?'

'A car had overturned on a hairpin bend. A mother and baby were trapped inside. When Zac came on the scene the only thing stopping it from tumbling down the gorge was a tree. Zac managed to pull the woman out before going back for the child.'

Jean-Claude was silent for a moment. 'As he was struggling to undo the baby seat, the car caught fire.'

'Did he get the baby out?'

'Yes, wrapped in a blanket. But Zac himself suffered third-degree burns. The doctors are very non-committal about his chances.'

Nanette turned and stared unseeingly as a plane landed and taxied down the runway, her thoughts in such turmoil she barely registered Jean-Claude's next words.

'The thing is, *ma chérie*, I know things are over between the two of you but in his delirious state he's been crying out for you. Can you bear the thought of holding a vigil at his bedside?'

CHAPTER ELEVEN

Nanette clutched Jean-Claude's hand tightly as they made their way into the Princess Grace Hospital in Monaco.

They found Zac in a small private room, wired up to a large piece of apparatus that was emitting a series of steady bleeps. Nanette swallowed hard as she looked at the heavily bandaged figure in the bed, unable to see any recognizable features and thinking it could be anyone.

Quietly, Nanette approached the bed.

'Zac?' she said softly. No response. Nanette turned questioningly to the nurse making notes of a reading off the machine.

'I'm sorry,' she said. 'Monsieur Ewart slipped into a coma an hour ago.'

Nanette glanced across at Jean-Claude.

'Why don't you sit down here?' he said, pulling a chair towards the side of the bed. 'I'll go and find us some coffee.'

Sitting there, gazing at Zac's motionless body, Nanette felt the tears welling up.

Through the years they had been together she had become hardened every time Zac climbed in a racing car, to expect the worst. She'd always known it was a dangerous sport where fatal accidents occurred despite all the modern safety measures and regulations. She'd learned to live with that fear, keeping her worries to herself and never mentioning them to Zac. He was doing a job he loved and living his life the way he wanted to and she'd reasoned it wasn't up to her to stop him.

To see him now, lying here in a hospital bed because he'd helped someone, was a cruel irony. Nanette bit her lip, determined not to cry at the unfairness of it all.

Tentatively, with her fingertips, she gently touched his bandaged hand, hoping against hope that he would open his eyes. However much he had hurt her, however much he had reviled her, she had once loved this man.

'I'm here, Zac,' she whispered. 'Please don't die.'

Jean-Claude returned with coffee and a sandwich for her. Moving away from the bed she gratefully accepted the plastic cup of steaming coffee, but shook her head at the sandwich he offered.

'Thank you, but I couldn't eat anything.'

A sudden discordant beep from the machine at Zac's side brought another nurse hurrying into the room, but seconds later the machine had settled back into its' steady bleep, bleep. The nurse shook her head in response to Nanette's worried look.

It was late evening before Jean-Claude persuaded Nanette it was time to go home.

'You need to get some sleep, *ma chérie*. And to eat something. If there's a change in Zac's condition overnight, the hospital will ring, and we'll come straight back, I promise,' Jean-Claude said. 'There is nothing you can do here.'

Glancing back as they left the room, Nanette sent a silent prayer winging in Zac's direction. 'Please, please wake up tomorrow. I want you to know how brave we all think you were.'

The lights were on in the villa as they drove up and Mathieu's car was parked in the driveway. Mathieu himself opened the front door to them.

'How's Zac?'

'He's been in a coma since this morning,' Jean-Claude replied quietly. 'What are you doing here? Do you have some news? A problem?'

Mathieu shook his head. 'No problem. But I wanted you to know that Boris was finally allowed to post bail today and he's out on remand. He's had to surrender his passport, of course, and must report to the police every day.'

He looked at his father. 'As far as he's concerned I'm still helping him so the pretence goes on for at least a few more days. I'm hoping that he's finally going to give me the name of his contact in Brazil who organizes the diamond smuggling. I can hand the completed file over to the police then.'

'Does Boris know about Zac?' Jean-Claude asked.

'Yes. He's asked me to let him know as soon as there is any change. He says he and Zac still have some unfinished business.'

'The stuff I put in the safe!' Nanette gasped. 'Do you think it's still there?'

Mathieu shrugged. 'Who knows? Maybe Zac moved it on before he left for the French Grand Prix. The unfinished business could be something to do with setting up *Vacances au Soleil*.'

Nanette spent a restless night in Jean-Claude's guest suite, unable to sleep, fearful that the phone would ring summoning her back to Zac's bedside.

Early morning sunlight was streaming in through the French doors of the sitting-room when she went downstairs. Jean-Claude was in the kitchen, listening to the news on the radio and preparing a breakfast tray for her.

'After you eat, I'll take you to the hospital,' he said, pouring her a large mug of coffee.

Nanette smiled her thanks and cupped her hands around the bowl. Information about Zac's accident was dominating the local radio stations' news bulletins and Nanette tensed as the voice of the woman he'd rescued came down the air. Praising his actions and calling him a hero, the woman sobbed with gratitude as she publicly thanked Zac for saving both her and her baby daughter and wished him a speedy recovery.

Silently, Jean-Claude leant across and switched off the radio. 'Breakfast, *ma chérie*, then we leave for the hospital.'

There was a small group of journalists hanging around the main entrance to the hospital as they arrived. One of them clearly recognized Nanette, but a glare from Jean-Claude and a sharp warning *'Non'* stopped him in the act of pointing his camera at her.

Zac's room was full of doctors and nurses and a worried Nanette and Jean-Claude had to wait outside for some time before they were allowed in.

'Is there any improvement in his condition?' Nanette asked.

'Monsieur Ewart had a stable night,' a young nurse informed them, 'but he remains unconscious.'

It was early afternoon when Zac stirred briefly and returned the gentle pressure as Nanette held his hand. That hardly felt squeeze filled Nanette with hope, but the rest of the afternoon passed without any further progress in Zac's condition.

At eight o'clock, as Jean-Claude suggested they should think about preparing to leave for the day, Zac unexpectedly opened his eyes and looked at them. Nanette felt her heart skip a beat as she smiled down at him.

'Hello Zac.'

'Nanette. Sorry. Shouldn't have lied.'

The words were spoken so softly that Nanette could barely hear them. She bent over him, anxious to catch anything else he might say.

'Please forgive me.'

'Of course, Zac. It's in the past. Just get well.'

Nanette glanced up as the machine started to emit a series of quick peeps and a nurse bustled in to check it.

'Would you mind leaving and coming back tomorrow please?'

As she turned to go, Zac murmured her name.

'Nanette – thank you.'

'I'll see you tomorrow, Zac.'

Moving towards the door where Jean-Claude was waiting for her, she turned to smile and mouthed 'goodbye' at Zac and caught the whispered words 'Be happy, Nanette' before his eyes closed again.

Jean-Claude held her hand tightly as he quickly led her past the journalists still waiting in the foyer.

'Any news?' one called out.

'*Non,*' Jean-Claude answered shortly.

To Nanette's surprise Jean-Claude didn't drive straight back to the villa instead he drove down to Cap D'Ail and parked the car.

'Come on, a walk along the beach to blow the cobwebs away,' he said. 'You need some fresh air before we go home for supper.'

Strolling along with Jean-Claude's arm around her shoulders holding her tight, Nanette felt strangely detached from reality. The last thirty-six hours had passed in a blur. Only now was she beginning to comprehend what had happened.

Zac's delirious ramblings had taken her to his bedside out of compassion and in remembrance of their past love. Now, as the breeze off the Mediterranean ruffled her hair, she thought about that love. How Zac's actions had changed it – how she had changed in the aftermath of her accident.

'If – when – Zac comes out of hospital, he will still need a lot of care for some time,' Jean-Claude said quietly, interrupting her thoughts. 'Round the clock attendance probably.'

Nanette nodded. 'I'll find the best for him. We'll nurse him back to health. Thank goodness he can afford all the care and help we need.'

At her words, Jean-Claude stopped walking and turned Nanette to face him. 'You are going to help nurse him?'

'No, not nurse him, but I'll organize his day-to-day needs.'

'How do you think he will react to the scars he is clearly going to have? Modern plastic surgery can do so much, but I'd hazard a guess that Zac's good looks have gone forever.'

'He's never been a bitter man – arrogant and self-seeking maybe,' Nanette answered slowly. 'I think once he knows the extent of his injuries, he'll get on with improving what he can and simply accept what he can't. He's always been very strong like that.'

'And you, *ma chérie*?' Jean-Claude gazed at her intently. 'How strong are you? How will you cope with a damaged Zac Ewart in your life?'

'JC, I can't just walk away from him.' Like he did to me, she added mentally.

'I wouldn't ask you to. I just don't want you to be hurt again.'

'I won't be, I promise.'

Nanette put a hand up and gently stroked Jean-Claude's face. 'Can I tell you something? Sitting at Zac's bedside I thought about you and me and wondered how I'd feel if it were you in that hospital bed.' Reaching up she kissed him. 'I couldn't bear it. I would really be hurting then.'

He hugged her tightly for several seconds before releasing her. 'Come on, let's walk.'

Dusk was falling as they returned to the villa. Mathieu met them at the door, his face serious.

'The hospital rang. Zac suffered a stroke shortly after you left. Nanette, I'm sorry, they did everything possible but they couldn't save him.'

Nanette lay on the airbed, her fingers dangling in the cool water as she drifted aimlessly around the pool. Jean-Claude had urged her to go for a swim but she simply didn't have the energy.

She'd felt so positive that night walking on the beach with Jean-Claude, watching the setting sun, believing against all odds that Zac was going to recover now he'd regained consciousness and making plans for his future care.

The numbness that had descended over her as Mathieu told them the sad news, had drained her of all rational thought and energy. Only Jean-Claude's quiet, loving presence had kept her focused on the things that needed to be done.

Together they had arranged the small immediate funeral service for Zac that would take place tomorrow in the church at the cemetery. They'd also begun to set the plans in motion for a big memorial service to be held in October at the end of the racing season.

And now an unknown Monsieur Mille had phoned wanting an urgent meeting with her that afternoon. Jean-Claude had been strangely reticent about the man, saying simply the name seemed familiar but he wasn't sure, and, as Monsieur Mille had declined to give details over the telephone, she'd have to wait and see what it was all about.

Reluctantly Nanette guided the airbed towards the pool steps. The mysterious Monsieur Mille would be here soon. She needed to shower and get dressed. Maybe she'd start to shake off this stupor after tomorrow when the saga of her and Zac would finally be laid to rest alongside his poor burned body.

Monsieur Mille, when Jean-Claude introduced them half an hour later, turned out to be a lawyer. Zac's lawyer.

'Mademoiselle Weston, I am here to offer my condolences and to tell you that you are the only beneficiary of Monsieur Ewart's estate.' He handed Nanette a legal document and an envelope containing a set of keys.

A stunned Nanette looked at him in disbelief as Jean-Claude took charge and began to question him.

'There is no mistake. Monsieur Ewart lodged his will with me three years ago with the instructions that in the event of his demise, I was to contact Mademoiselle Weston, with the news and offer her my services.'

'But three years ago. . . .' Nanette's voice trailed off.

'I believe you had a bad car accident about that time,' the lawyer said. 'Monsieur Ewart was concerned for you.'

He stood up and held out his business card. 'I will leave you to read Monsieur Ewart's will. If you have any questions this is my number. These things take time, but you will need to come to my office to sign papers – perhaps next month.'

Nanette stayed in the sitting-room while Jean-Claude saw the lawyer out, her thoughts in turmoil. Why hadn't Zac changed his will? Was it his way of trying to make amends? Or was it just a mistake on his part? Whatever the reason, it was too late now.

Her fingers were shaking as she unfolded the heavy document. There was no mistaking her name in bold letters six or seven lines down the page identifying her as the beneficiary of Zac Ewart's estate. Silently she handed the paper to Jean-Claude when he returned.

Pole Position, the apartment in Fontvieille – those were the keys the lawyer had thoughtfully put in the envelope – and a bank account were now hers.

'You're going to be a wealthy woman,' Jean-Claude said.

'I don't deserve this,' she said, looking up at Jean-Claude. 'I certainly don't want it.'

'I don't think you can refuse,' Jean-Claude said gently. 'But once you've signed all the legal documents you can do what you like with it.'

'I'll give it away then.'

John-Claude regarded her thoughtfully.

'The package you put in the safe – I think we should take a look and see if it's still there. I don't want you implicated in Zac's criminal activities simply because you now own the yacht.'

'I need some fresh air – shall we go now?' Nanette asked. 'Get it over with. I'll just get my bag.'

Nanette's mobile phone rang as they were leaving the villa. It was Vanessa.

'I just wanted you to know that I'm coming down for the funeral tomorrow. Mathieu is meeting me at Nice tonight and I've booked a room at the Columbus.'

'Are the twins coming too?'

'No. Ralph is taking them down to his parents in the country for a couple of days. I thought they were a bit young – although Pierre in particular is terribly upset about Zac. I think he was looking forward to boasting that the Formula One World Champion was a friend.'

There was a pause before Vanessa said, 'You coping? We'll have a long talk tomorrow.'

'Yes,' Nanette answered. 'I'm coping and there's a lot to talk about when you get here.'

The harbour was busy as Nanette and Jean-Claude made their way to the yacht. As they walked, they saw *Mediterranean Wanderer* negotiating its way to a quayside berth, scores of cruise passengers lining her decks for their first look at Monaco.

Several police cars were parked along the embankment road effectively blocking a lane of traffic. A loud blaring of car horns from exasperated drivers forced into gridlock competed with the noisy siren from the liner as it warned smaller craft to get out of its way.

Nanette nudged Jean-Claude. 'Isn't that Boris sitting at that café? Oh, and there's Mathieu.'

Jean-Claude followed her gaze. 'Wasn't *Mediterranean Wanderer* on Zac's list? Maybe Boris is waiting to meet someone. As long as Mathieu isn't doing his dirty work for him.' Jean-Claude gave an anxious look in his son's direction.

'Shall we wait and see?'

Jean-Claude shook his head. 'No. I have to do as Mathieu says and trust him. Let's look at the safe.'

Phil, the skipper, was alone on board and eager to offer his condolences to Nanette.

'It's hard to believe. Such a tragedy. Away from the race track too,' he said. 'Have you heard anything about what happens next?'

'The funeral is tomorrow – very low-key. We're planning a memorial service in October,' Nanette answered, unwilling to tell Phil yet that she was the new owner. He'd find out soon enough.

'Remember those things I had to put in Zac's private safe? I need to see if they are still there. We won't be five minutes,' Nanette said, taking Jean-Claude's hand, compelling him to follow her into the master cabin, where she closed the door.

'The time for secrets is over.'

Kneeling in front of the cupboard in the bathroom she took out the towels and the shelf. Carefully she punched the number into the combination lock and pulled the door open. The package and the gun were still there.

A muttered 'Blast' escaped from Jean-Claude. '*Désolé*. I was hoping that Zac had already moved the stuff by now. OK, the gun isn't too big a problem – we can simply hand it in to the authorities. It's not illegal to own a gun. The package though does give us a problem. We certainly can't leave it here.'

'I'll put it in my bag, shall I?' Nanette asked. 'Take it back to the villa and talk to Mathieu. He may be able to suggest something.'

'*D'accord*,' Jean-Claude said, picking up the gun and making sure the safety catch was on before he slipped it into the inside pocket of his jacket.

Phil was waiting for them in the stern. 'Safe empty then?' he asked.

'Yes,' Nanette said. He wasn't to know that it was empty because the main contents were now nestling in her bag.

Passengers from the cruise liner were thronging the pavements as Nanette and Jean-Claude stepped ashore. Traffic along the harbour road was still at a virtual standstill and a large crowd were watching the *gendarmes* frog-march somebody off the *Mediterranean Wanderer*.

Passing the pavement café where they'd seen Boris earlier, Nanette glanced around in time to see him disappearing into the crowd, with a thoughtful Mathieu watching him go.

Mathieu raised a languid hand in greeting as he saw them and walked towards them.

'Cruz has been arrested. I expect things to start happening now,' he said. 'You're looking very serious, Nanette. Has something happened?'

'We need you to come up to the villa,' Jean-Claude answered before Nanette could. 'We have something to discuss with you urgently.'

Zac's funeral service was as private as Nanette had hoped it would be. Altogether there were just nine people in the congregation to hear the vicar's eulogy of Zac's life and the brave actions that had taken it away from him.

The Oliviers had travelled down and were seated with the woman whose baby and life Zac had saved. Phil was there and Monsieur Mille slipped into a seat at the back. Mathieu and Vanessa sat behind Nanette and Jean-Claude.

Listening to the words of praise for a man who had been a part of her life for several years and who would continue to be a never forgotten presence by virtue of his legacy to her, Nanette found herself fighting back the tears. Silently Jean-Claude handed her a handkerchief.

After the short service Jean-Claude invited everybody back to the villa. The Oliviers, Monsieur Mille and the rescued woman all declined, citing various reasons but Phil accepted.

'So, if the rumours are to be believed,' he said, awkwardly, as Nanette offered him a drink, 'you're my new boss. Are you going to keep *Pole Position*?'

'Phil, I'm sorry, but it's too soon to know. I haven't decided what I'm going to do about a lot of things, *Pole Position* included. As soon as I do, I promise I'll keep you informed. In the meantime, you're still her skipper.'

Across the room she could see Mathieu in earnest conversation with Jean-Claude and Vanessa, but it wasn't until after Phil had left and the four of them were alone that Nanette heard what they were talking about.

'Boris has had his bail revoked,' Jean-Claude told her.

'Once the police got Cruz into custody yesterday he sang like a bird,' Mathieu explained. 'Apparently he was more than just a courier. He was able to supply missing contact names, routes and some other information the police needed.

They didn't wait for Boris to do his daily sign-in – they re-arrested him last night and got a judge to revoke his bail.'

'Did Cruz implicate Zac in any way?' Nanette asked quietly.

Mathieu shook his head. 'No.'

Nanette breathed a sigh of relief before asking, 'What did you do with the shampoo?'

'Told the police where it had come from and handed it over. Don't worry,' he continued, seeing her anxious look. 'It won't be used as evidence. And, seeing there are enough people willing to testify against Boris, now he's in custody and can't threaten them anymore, I've "lost" my dossier on Zac's activities. I can't see the police bothering with a dead hero. I shall have to give evidence against Boris, of course.'

'Does he know yet that you were double-crossing him?' Jean-Claude asked.

'No. The police are keeping that little bit of information for the trial. I'm just glad it's all over and I can get back to a normal life,' he said, looking at his father. 'I really hated deceiving you.'

'Now I know the truth I have to say I'm proud of you,' Jean-Claude said. 'You did the right thing.'

There was a short pause before Jean-Claude spoke again.

'Does getting back to a normal life mean getting more involved in my business as well as your own? I was hoping that we could combine them both, with me taking a sabbatical for a few months.'

'Shall we have a business meeting tomorrow morning and start to sort things out?' Mathieu said.

Jean-Claude hesitated. 'I was going to suggest I took Nanette down to Zac's apartment but when we get back would be fine.'

'JC, don't worry about that,' Nanette said. 'I'll drive myself down. Leave you free to discuss business with Mathieu. Vanessa will come with me, won't you?' Nanette turned to her friend.

'Of course.'

'Are you sure?' Jean-Claude asked.

'Definitely. My convertible has been sitting in your garage far too long. It's time I got mobile again.'

Nanette parked in one of the underground car-parks near the circus tent in Fontvielle.

'Do you mind walking to the apartment from here?' she asked Vanessa. 'You can tell me how the plans for the co-operative are coming on as we go.'

She winced as a particularly noisy helicopter came in over the Mediterranean to land at the shoreline heliport, just yards away from where they were standing.

'I'm still looking for sponsors for the first year. Flying down here for Zac's funeral was the main reason I'm here but it isn't the only reason. I need to talk to you about Fruits of the Forest.'

Nanette looked at Vanessa and waited.

'I know you said you didn't want to be involved because you were going to be spending more and more time down here and I planned to run Fruits from the UK. Well, I've changed my mind. Ralph and I are going to relocate here. He can work from anywhere, the twins like their school and seeing more of Mathieu – and, of course, the co-operative will benefit from the tax breaks Monaco can give. So, will you change your mind?'

'Oh Vanessa,' Nanette said. 'I'm sorry the answer is still no, but I do know someone who needs a job and who would be perfect. Evie. Her boss got caught up in all this smuggling business and she lost her job recently.'

'This Boris Takyanov certainly spread his business tentacles widely, didn't he?' Vanessa said. 'Unbelievable that so deep in the jungle, we should cross the same criminal organization that Mathieu was investigating. Apart from Ralph's accident, the only time I was truly scared, was when the villagers accused us of putting the evil eye on them because of Maksim Takyanov's failure to honour their deal.'

'I find the fact that Zac got taken in unbelievable,' Nanette said. 'And trying to involve me in *Vacances au Soleil* to give it respectability was despicable.' She shook her head. 'I just took it as the final proof that he didn't give a hoot about me but then, this happens,' and she looked up reflectively at the apartment building where they were now standing.

The concierge welcomed them politely, pointed out which lift they needed to take for Apartment 210 on the twelfth floor and returned to tending the vast pots of lilies that graced the foyer.

Stepping out of the lift and inserting the key in the apartment door, Nanette shivered.

Vanessa glancing at her asked, 'You OK?'

'I'm fine. Probably reaction to the last few days. This whole Zac thing still feels unreal.'

'We don't have to do this today, do we?' Vanessa asked. 'You don't have to rush into sorting things out.'

'No, but I need to make a start,' Nanette said, before resolutely turning the key.

'This is surreal,' she murmured, looking around the

sparsely furnished sitting-room. It was full of things she recognized from Zac's old apartment – things they had chosen together.

The two white leather settees facing each other across the glass topped coffee table, the music centre, the Persian rug, the grand piano from Zac's grandmother. All brought back poignant memories of her time with him.

She brushed away a tear before walking across and picking up a silver-framed photo standing on the piano. It was one of Zac standing in the cockpit of *Pole Position* looking relaxed and happy.

'I've never thanked you properly for having the twins for me and coming back to Monaco,' Vanessa said unexpectedly. 'I know it was a difficult decision for you to return.'

'I'm glad I came. Getting my memory back, clearing things up between Zac and me – imagine how I would have felt if Zac had died and we'd never talked about the accident.'

Nanette took one last look at the photo and gently replaced it on the piano before turning to face Vanessa.

'You did me a favour in more ways than one by going up the Amazon for five months.' Nanette smiled at her friend as she moved towards the master bedroom door. 'It's thanks to you I've now got Jean-Claude in my life.'

'The rain forest was such a great experience. I can't tell you how much it changed the way I look at things,' Vanessa said quietly.

Nanette barely heard her friend as she looked at Zac's bedside table. Yet another silver-framed photo – and this time Nanette couldn't stop the tears from coursing down her cheeks as she looked at it.

Taken the night they got engaged at a party in the

Automobile Club in Monaco, she and Zac were standing with their arms entwined in the traditional manner, toasting each other with champagne, her engagement ring sparkling in the camera flash.

'Do you think Zac's got any tea? I think we could both do with a cup,' Vanessa said. 'Come on, let's inspect the kitchen.' Gently she led Nanette out of the bedroom.

By the time Vanessa had found and made a pot of tea, Nanette had stopped crying.

'I'm sorry. I thought I was all cried out over Zac Ewart but apparently not.' She took a deep breath. 'Such a waste but life moves on. At least his reputation as a brilliant racing driver will remain intact. He'll never have to face the criminal charges that Boris and the others will.' She took a sip of tea.

'This is a great apartment,' Vanessa said looking around. 'Are you going to keep it and live here?'

'I'll probably sell it. Can't see myself living here somehow. If I keep it, I'll rent it out. Oh!' Nanette said, looking at Vanessa. 'In the meantime – why don't you and Ralph make it your base when you move down here?'

After Vanessa had gone back to the UK and he'd had his business meeting with Mathieu, Jean-Claude insisted they enjoyed the few remaining days of Nanette's official holiday doing things together.

On the last day they drove up into the back country and had lunch in a village square sitting beneath the shade of an ancient plane tree.

As the waiter placed their tomato and mozzarella salad in front of them, Jean-Claude glanced across at her.

'I'm so happy you've decided not to rush back to the UK

with Vanessa. I love having you around.'

Nanette smiled at him as he picked up her hand and squeezed it.

'Have you thought about what you are going to do with your legacy yet?'

'I've done nothing but think about it,' Nanette answered. 'There is one idea floating around in my brain I want to talk to you about.'

'Do you still want to give it all away?'

Nanette shook her head. 'No, that was a silly idea. I'll keep it, but I do want to do something useful with it if I can.' She poured herself a glass of water from the carafe the waiter had placed on the table before continuing, 'I was wondering about *Pole Position*. We could have some fun with her, or I could sell her and invest the money. What do you think?'

'Any ideas where you'd invest such a large sum? She's worth at least two million dollars,' Jean-Claude said.

'I hadn't realized she was worth that much. But that would be fantastic.' Nanette smiled at him hesitantly, trying to gauge his reaction to her next words.

'I was thinking of offering to sponsor Fruits of the Forest for the first year in Zac's name. Even if it's registered as a charity it's going to need a large injection of cash to get it off the ground.'

'Not your conventional investment then?' Jean-Claude said smiling. 'Well, it won't make you a fortune but it would make a difference to a lot of people's lives in the rain forest.'

'From what Monsieur Mille tells me Zac's left me a small fortune – I don't need to make another one,' Nanette said quietly. 'Right that's decision number one: next week I'll find a broker and put *Pole Position* up for sale.'

Nanette stopped talking to watch a woman pushing a buggy with a sleeping baby and holding a little boy by the hand pass their table. The sleeping baby reminded her of Dylan; they were about the same age.

'And decision number two?' Jean-Claude probed.

'If I'm staying in Monaco I need to find somewhere to live. I don't want to live in Zac's apartment in Fontvielle; besides I've already offered it to Vanessa and Ralph in the short term.'

'What is wrong with living at the villa with me?' Jean-Claude demanded. 'The guest room has never had a more welcome occupant.'

'I don't want to get in the way,' Nanette said. 'I was only supposed to be here for a holiday.'

'*Ma chérie*, you know how I feel about you. You will never be in my way. You stay at the villa. That's decision number two dealt with.' Heedless of the other diners, Jean-Claude leant forward and gently kissed her.

Later as they were making their way back to the car they passed the mother and her two children playing in the park alongside the church. The small boy miss-kicked his ball which landed at Jean-Claude's feet.

Jean-Claude promptly kicked it back and for several moments he and the small boy had an animated kick around while Nanette talked to the mother.

'That took me back,' Jean-Claude said, when they eventually waved goodbye to the toddler. 'I used to play football with Mathieu years ago.'

'You obviously like *les enfants*,' Nanette said.

'Before things went wrong with Amelia I'd always hoped Mathieu would have a sibling.' Jean-Claude shrugged. 'I've always regretted that.'

'Well, it's not too late, is it?' Nanette said. 'I'm sure Mathieu would still adore having a half-brother or sister,' she teased, smiling at him. A look of incredulous wonder crossed Jean-Claude's face as Nanette leaned forward and kissed him.

On the night of the Red Cross Gala, one of the biggest social events of the Monte Carlo season, Nanette carefully slipped the wisp of pale-lemon chiffon that was her evening dress over her head. She was really looking forward to this evening.

It came at the end of a few very busy weeks: overseeing the sorting out of Zac's affairs; selling *Pole Position*; helping Vanessa and Ralph move into the Fontvielle apartment and persuading Vanessa to let her use the proceeds from the sale of *Pole Position* to sponsor Fruits of the Forest for a year.

'Are you sure? It's an awful lot of money to be virtually giving away.'

'Absolutely positive. Zac bought *Pole Position* about eight years ago and I'm fairly certain it was with his winnings and sponsorship deals, but who knows?' She shrugged her shoulders.

'If, and we don't know for certain how long Zac was involved with Boris, any of this money I have now inherited came from smuggling Brazilian diamonds or money laundering, then this is a way of giving it back legally.'

Nanette slipped her feet into her high-heeled gold sandals and did them up. Her diamond encrusted watch Jean-Claude had given her was already on her wrist and she picked up her beaded evening clutch bag.

Jean-Claude was waiting for her in the sitting-room.

'You look beautiful,' he said, taking her in his arms. 'The belle of the ball. Come on, the others are waiting. Let's party.'

Jean-Claude had invited Vanessa and Ralph to join their party for the evening – Mathieu and Evie were the other couple. Mathieu had met Evie when she'd started working for Fruits of the Forest and to Nanette's secret delight, the two were rapidly becoming an item around the Principality.

The whole of Monte Carlo seemed to be in festive mood that evening. Champagne flowed, people wined and dined and everybody was on their feet dancing for hours.

Towards midnight, she and Jean-Claude mingled with the other party-goers as they all made their way out on to the terrace in a brief pause in the festivities before the fireworks began. Vanessa and Ralph had managed to save them a good viewing position and Mathieu and Evie soon joined them.

Nanette, standing there with her friends and Jean-Claude's arm around her shoulders, looked around contentedly. Tomorrow she and Jean-Claude would be flying to a very different world when they left to visit the UK for Dylan's christening. Two contrasting worlds, but both now very much a part of her life.

Jean-Claude had been delighted when Patsy had phoned and asked him to be a godparent with Nanette and had been planning all sorts of surprises for the unsuspecting Dylan.

The whoosh of the first warning rocket and everyone looked skywards, except Jean-Claude who gently drew Nanette towards him.

Surprised she looked at him as he took both her hands in his. '*Ma chérie*, will you marry me?'

The sky exploded with thousands of silver stars in time with her heart as Nanette whispered a tremulous, 'Yes please.'

Jean-Claude slipped a ring on her finger while more fiery flashes of gold, silver, red and blue filled the sky over Monte

Carlo before showering down into the Mediterranean.

Surrendering herself to Jean-Claude's arms, Nanette knew beyond all doubt that his love was her second, true, legacy from France.